D1148138

WITHDRAWN FROM
BROMLEY LIBRARIES

Published by Curious Fox, an imprint of Capstone Global Library Limited,
264 Banbury Road, Oxford, OX2 7DY – Registered company number: 6695582

www.curious-fox.com

Illustrations by Brann Garvey

ISBN 978 1 78202 598 6

20 19 18 17 16
10 9 8 7 6 5 4 3 2 1

A CIP catalogue for this book is available from the British Library.

Printed and bound in UK

HOW TO STAGE A CATASTROPHE

by Rebecca Donnelly

Curious Fox
a capstone company-publishers for children

FOR MARY

(That's not an acronym, but if it was,
it would stand for something awesome.)

Presenting the story of how we saved the
Juicebox Theatre.
(It's not cheating to tell you that.
I don't want you to worry, that's all.)

Ready? Okay, curtain up.

Part 1

Act I

SCENE ONE

(In a play, every scene is supposed to have some kind of point to it. Like, a major thing happens, or some really important secret is revealed. In this scene, I'm trying to figure out how to earn enough money to buy a karaoke machine.

Also, every scene has a setting. Right now it's my kitchen, but we'll change the set later so you can see other stuff like all the brown and tan houses on Hatahatchee Street, which is where I live now. It used to be part of an Air Force base, but when they shut down the base, they sold the houses and left a hundred and twenty-two gallons of brown and tan paint in the garage of the house that we bought. Now when someone needs a touch-up on their paint job, they call my dad. Everyone's got a brown or tan house around here. Only Mr Jameson's house next door is yellow, but that, believe it or not, is a sad story.)

Picture an empty stage. Now, that stage can't stay empty, because no one's going to sit around and watch that forever. So you see a kid – that's me – coming on from stage right. That's your left, if you're in the audience.

This kid, me, is in his kitchen on a Saturday morning

in June. I'm not really an actor, though. Think of me as the director here, so when the doorbell rings in a second and my best friend, Folly, shows up with his dog Francolina, it's because I told him to.

That's what it means to be the director. You get to figure out all the blocking, which means you tell everyone where to go onstage. That's why one day I'm going to do what Ruben does at the Juicebox and direct real plays. He says maybe after seventh grade, I can be his assistant director. Right now I just handle all the props.

Picture a freestanding door off to stage left (that's right to you), and there's another kid and a scruffy-looking orange dog (sorry, Frankie) standing there. The kid's looking all business-like, which is represented by the bow tie clipped to his shirt and by the briefcase. He's also looking a bit sick with love, which is represented by the heavy sighs and this dreamy, fluttery thing he's doing with his eyelashes.

The flutters are for my sister May.

I open the door, and Folly practically falls into me. He recovers himself like a pro. "You ready to go to Mr J's?"

We have some business next door in Mr Jameson's chicken coop. Folly collects the eggs every day, and on Saturdays he sells them around the neighbourhood while I clean out the coop.

"In a second," I say. "Come and have an old doughnut."

Folly straightens his bow tie. "Not if you paid me to. A man's body is like a bank vault. Whatever he puts in there is being saved up for later."

"Zap Zapter?" I guess. Zap Zapter writes these books Folly loves about business and selling stuff and How to Live Right. They're full of strategies and acronyms and all kinds of motivational sayings. Folly's read dozens of them, even the ones from twenty years ago that he's picked up second-hand. He's probably memorized every word in them, which means he's got something to say for every situation. That can come in handy.

"TZK," says Folly.

The Zap Knows. That's one of his favourite acronyms. And you can't ever doubt the wisdom of Zap Zapter if Folly's less than nine miles away.

I pick up a pink-sprinkle doughnut from the box that Gram brought home from karaoke night at the Pick n' Play. I suspect Dad got hold of the box, because he'll eat any doughnut besides the ones with sprinkles. I'm about to take a bite when, wouldn't you know it, here comes May.

Everyone says May is beautiful, and she might be. I don't pay attention to that kind of thing. I was supposed to write a poem about her for Family Week in fifth grade, but all I could write was: *She's got eyes like a hundred dewdrops and long, long fingers for getting into other people's business.*

"Sidney," May says, and she drifts over to me on a little cloud of fluffy slippers. "I don't know what you and Orpheus are doing in this kitchen with that ratty orange dog and doughnut sprinkles in your teeth, but you'd better not be cooking up any dumb schemes. You have real work to do."

Folly's real name is Orpheus, but after reading the one hundred and twenty-seven books of Zap Zapter, he decided he needed to give himself a good, memorable name. I thought he had a pretty good name to start with, but it's not my decision.

May is going to be sorry she was so mean to Folly when he strikes it rich and he drives his raspberry-coloured BMW with the top down to the opening night of my latest Broadway show.

Folly doesn't have a BMW, but it's on his executive list. His Pap-Pap drives one, and he's on the board of the Gainesville African-American Chamber of Commerce and owns all the Shop Fast supermarkets in Alachua County.

"Good morning, May," says Folly in his deepest voice. He smiles, and I can tell he wants her to see *he* doesn't have doughnut sprinkles in his teeth. "I'm starting my newest business enterprise today."

Folly's been starting business enterprises since the day he tried to sell his finger-painted self-portrait to his own mother in kindergarten. That's how she tells it. Folly says he was just trying to get her in on a good investment while prices were low.

May goes back a step and takes us both in. "As long as I still get that dozen eggs, Bow Tie, I don't care what you do."

May just can't be kind. I told her not to call Folly that, but Folly said he'd wear that bow tie every day of his life if she wanted him to. Not out loud, but down in his heart, I could tell that's what he was saying. Besides, he's convinced

14

he's going to earn Zap Zapter's Golden Bow Tie Award one day, which is kind of like the business version of getting a gold star on your maths test. He says wearing a bow tie reminds him of his purpose in life.

So besides being a fifteen-year-old tyrant, May is the meringue queen. Don't ask me why, but that's the only kind of food she likes to make. Pure sugar and egg whites, with one tiny chocolate chip right on top. Whatever eggs I get from Mr Jameson for cleaning his chicken coop go right to her, and she goes right to the kitchen, and by the time I get there, there's nothing left but a bowl of yolk. She doesn't even eat meringues. Too much sugar. Whenever she makes them, she hops on her bike with a whole basket of them and rides off like she's delivering human organs and she doesn't want the ice to melt. I don't know where she goes, but May wouldn't ride a bike in this heat for just any reason. I tried following her once, but when she turned out of our neighbourhood onto Longleaf Parkway towards town, I lost my nerve. That's a long, straight road, and she would have seen me behind her.

"Actually," Folly says, pulling at his bow tie again, "me and Sid are going into business together. We're expanding from agricultural products into, uh, into other lines."

"We are?" This is a surprise to me, since I can't really say I'm in the agricultural product business. Unless you count chicken poop as a product, and I don't know if you can count that. I wouldn't.

"We are."

I'm hoping Folly's new scheme goes better than the one he tried last summer. His Pap-Pap used to sell newspapers when he was a kid, and Folly thought it was his duty to follow in his footsteps. But newspaper companies don't pay kids to deliver the papers anymore. Folly bought some for a quarter each and then set up a table in front of his house. He charged forty cents because, as he says, you have to make a profit. But you can't make a profit if no one buys anything from you. He sold one to his mum and one to Gram and that was the end of that.

Before I can find out more about this business enterprise we're starting, the scene gets a little busier.

My little sister, Penelope, is the next one onstage. She's still got her PJs on, and her pirate patch over her left eye. That means she's found treasure. She's been wearing it over her left eye a lot lately. As small as she is, she looks like about half a pirate, that's all. Actually, with her hair in a little pink bow right on top of her head, she looks like this Yorkie dog I saw on a box of dog biscuits at the Pet Palace. Only I'd never say so because I don't want to get bitten.

She opens her mouth to say something, but I cut her off. "No, I haven't done Mr Jameson's chickens yet. You'll get your feather when I'm done."

Pen the Half-Pirate is forever gathering feathers and things and burying them out in the woods like treasure. You might think she'd dig up some dangerous stuff, because this used to be a military base, but where we live was the old family housing area. The rest of the base is being turned

16

into a business park or something, which makes Folly's heart flutter just like his eyelashes.

Pen peers at me with her one good eye and gets herself a slice of bread. She chews it ten times each bite. That's something Gram said is good for the digestion. Does that mean doughnuts are good for the digestion, too? I don't think Gram would steer me wrong. She's the one who told me to brush my teeth with bicarbonate of soda to get them sparkly white for when I'm a real director.

Now May's glaring at us like a rain cloud with a grudge, and Folly pulls at his tie again. It's a Folly trademark. I'm about to run for it, but long-fingered May yanks me by the collar. You didn't think people really did that, did you? But May's got real theatrical flair. She holds on to me like we're doing one of Ruben's theatre exercises, the one where you have to do a whole scene without ever letting go of your partner.

"You'd better work as fast as you can. When you're done we're driving down to the theatre for my rehearsal."

Her rehearsal? Every kid in the company is rehearsing something for the variety show fundraiser tonight, but to hear May, you wouldn't think anything else was going on besides her love affair with the spotlight. She won't even call it the Juicebox anymore, because she says that makes it sound like a place for babies.

I wriggle free from May's pincers. I'm good at that. "So what's our newest business–" I start to say to Folly, but May cuts me off.

"Sidney Horatio Camazzola. I'm going to stuff your ugly head in a basket and throw you out the front door if you don't get over to Mr Jameson's house before I count to three-quarters. One-quarter."

"But you wouldn't hurt a poor orphan, would you?"

"Ruben gave us that scene to practise last week, Sidney, and you were terrible at it then, too. Two-quarters."

"That's one-half, May. You could've just said one-half."

"Three–"

And I am gone. But not because I really think May's going to have any luck trying get this head inside a basket, orphan or not. I'm wilier than any basket ever made. I leave double fast because I want to eat my leftover karaoke pink-sprinkle doughnut in peace, and where there is May, there is never any peace.

* * *

You might be wondering why I didn't say a word about any karaoke machine during that whole scene, if that was supposed to be the main point. Well, you just weren't looking. It's called internal motivation. I was thinking about it the whole time.

If this was a real play, I would've given you a programme at the start of it. It's got advertising and stuff in it and it tells you about the play, the director and the cast. So why don't you take a look at the programme now, while I'm walking over to Mr Jameson's.

PROGRAMME

The name of the play:
I don't know that yet. I'm still working on it.

The director:
Sidney Camazzola. Sidney *Horatio* Camazzola.

Location:
Hatahatchee, Florida, between the old bombing range and the Blue Crab Bay. Pretty much the greatest town anywhere, ever.

Time:
Time's a funny thing. Let's just say, Right now.

Act I

SCENE TWO

(I know, I didn't get to the cast part, but there wasn't time. Mr Jameson lives just next door.

The front of Mr Jameson's house looks a lot like the front of my house except it's yellow, like I said. The back of it looks the same, too, except his has chickens.)

Remember how I said this is Act One? They do that with plays. You have three acts, and it's like: here's a problem, here's how all the characters try to fix the problem and sometimes run into more problems, and here's how the problem gets fixed. We're about to learn more about the problem.

I cross our dead grass to Mr Jameson's garden, and Folly and Frankie go around the long way, up the path, because it looks more professional.

"Good morning, Mr Camazzola. That's one good-looking hairdo," Mr Jameson calls from his shady front porch, where he's parked his wheelchair.

Yes, it is one good-looking hairdo. I cut it myself last week, back when I was being an orphan. Sometimes I keep doing Ruben's exercises even after we leave the theatre, because I need to know my stuff if I'm going to direct one day.

Mum offered to cut my hair for me, but I told her orphans can't let their mums do things for them. That's what it means to be an orphan.

"Makes him look like a quail," Folly says in a way that only Folly could say it, without making me want to trip him.

Mr Jameson wipes at the back of his neck. Even this early in the day it's hot and humid. "Mr King. How's business?" He tips up his hat, the one Gram calls a fisherman's cap.

Folly gives Mr Jameson a slick grin. I can see how he might look a lot like Mr Jameson when he's grown up. Not just because they have the same dark brown skin or because neither one of them goes around looking like a quail. They have the same kind of confidence and sunny attitude that I'm happy just to be around. "Business is good, sir. It'd be even better if you could get some more chickens."

"No can do," says Mr Jameson. "I already have more chickens than I'm supposed to. The rules say you can have up to twenty. I'm risking some kind of official chicken seizure as it is."

"Chicken seizure?" I say, and Mr Jameson nods.

"It's a terrible thing. The mayor herself has to come and

chase down every one of the chickens and put it into a cage. That's a sight too tragic to behold."

I don't want to see Mr Jameson's chickens get put in a cage and taken away, but I wouldn't mind seeing the mayor of Hatahatchee chasing them around for a while. I don't think Mr Jameson's being serious, but you would never know from how straight his expression is.

Folly gets a wad of money from his briefcase. Something funny happens when Folly talks about money. It always comes out sounding like this:

ASSETS	LIABILITIES
$12.00	$6.00
PROFIT	$6.00

He calls that a balance sheet, and if you ask Folly what a balance sheet is, he'll say it's a company's complete financial picture, all at once, for one moment in time. Folly probably sleeps on balance sheets. He has a revenue stream running where his bloodstream ought to be. I'm not saying he's a cold-hearted cash machine, but I think if he could line his shirts with dollar bills, he'd do it just to feel them crinkling all day long. I bet if I watch him close enough, one day I'll see him spit out a nickel.

I can't understand a word of what he's saying. Mr Jameson gets right to the point. He says, "What are the takings this week, Mr King?"

"Twelve total, six for you and six for me. And your receipt."

He holds out a piece of paper with a little flourish. Mr Jameson doesn't make him give receipts, but Folly likes to practise writing in his business hand.

He's always been like that. He worked out last year that Mr Jameson doesn't need twenty-seven chickens' worth of eggs all for himself. He was practically drowning in eggs before I brought Folly over one day when I went to clean the coop. He gave us each a dozen at the end of the day, and said there were more where all those came from. Folly said then and there that he was going to help Mr Jameson out and sell them around to the neighbours, and make a little money himself.

You're thinking it's a real shame that I do the dirty work and Folly gets all the glory and the money? Well, that's okay. Folly deserves some glory, and I know he can use some money. His mum was expecting a big pay-off from an investment she made last year, but the pay-off never came. Now Folly has to earn his allowance, which he calls his petty cash. He keeps it in an old cash box under his bed and writes himself receipts whenever he takes any money out of it. What do I make for cleaning the coop? Just that dozen eggs I give to May. I'm a real charitable institution, but not because Mr Jameson uses a wheelchair, but because no one will let me charge him anything. Mum says I will be amply rewarded for helping out a neighbour, but I don't think she means rewarded with money.

Wait. I do get something besides the eggs.

Every Saturday after I clean the chicken coop and put all the poop on to Mr Jameson's compost pile, he brings a jug of iced tea out onto the porch and says he'll answer one question. You don't think that's a good deal for me? You must not have a neighbour like Mr Jameson. He was in the Marines for four years, and he knows everything there is to know about web design and the University of Florida Gators, and a lot else besides. I can ask him anything that doesn't involve a) swearing or b) the birds and the bees (meaning he does not want to talk to me about the kinds of things May says I'm going to learn about in health class later anyway). The birds and the bees also include asking questions about his personal life with Mrs Jameson before the accident. No problem, I told him, because I don't want to know that anyway.

But I can ask him stuff like how does he drive his car with those hand controls instead of the pedals, and how the heck does he get his arms to be as big around as a python with a whole rabbit in its gut like I saw at the Pet Palace once? When I asked him that one he showed me some of his workout routine with weights and stuff, and then he let me hold one of the weights and I almost fell over backwards when I tried to lift it above my head.

(We're going back in time a little bit. It's hard to do a flashback in a play. You don't have that wavy-screen thing they use on TV, but I suppose you could use dry ice or something.)

A few weeks ago I wanted to know what Mr Jameson's favourite thing is that he owns, and he went right inside and came out with a glittery yellow scarf. It looked like something Gram might wear on her singing nights.

"Mrs Jameson was wearing this when I talked to her for the first time," he said. "She was playing Billie Holiday in the high school's spring musical." I could see why maybe that would make something pretty special.

"Your favourite thing is a scarf?"

"I cheated. That's my second-favourite thing. My favourite thing is a photograph, but I can't show it to you."

"Oh," I said. "The birds and the bees."

"No, Sid, I don't keep pictures like that around. I'm talking about the best picture ever taken of the lovely Jocelyn Jameson, and I just can't find it. Can you imagine that? My favourite thing in the whole world, and I don't even know where it is."

And right then, even though he looked like he could arm-wrestle a rhinoceros without any trouble, and in every other way he was as neat as a pin and completely in control, Mr Jameson looked like he was going to cry.

(Back to the present.)

The chickens live in the coop Mr and Mrs Jameson built when they moved in three years ago, back when Gram

26

called them the two lovebirds. Mr and Mrs Jameson, that is, not the chickens. When they bought the house next door to us, they got to work right away planting vegetables and flowers, and Mr Jameson hung a porch swing for them to sit on in the evenings. They invited us over to swing on their porch, too, and for barbecues and to light colour-changing spinning eyeballs and sparklers on the Fourth of July.

I would build a set to show you what it looked like, except that it makes me feel sick inside when I think about how they only finished painting their house sunshine yellow two weeks before the car accident.

(Okay, we're in the past again.)

Dad was down the street painting windowsills at the time, and he watched it happen. He said that van must have driven out of the fourth dimension, because it wasn't there and then in the blink of an eye it went straight into the Jamesons' car. They were just trying to go and see a play in Pensacola.

Mr Jameson broke his spinal cord and stayed in the hospital for two months. Mrs Jameson never made it home.

I meant it when I said it was a sad story. But one thing I know about stories from seeing so many of them on the stage is that they have a way of changing on you. You think one thing's going to happen, and then something else happens instead, and something that starts out sad ends up being okay. So I'm going to keep things moving along here, otherwise there's no chance for that to happen.

(Back to the present. And it smells . . . not great.)

Do you want to get a look inside a chicken coop that has twenty-seven chickens and one rotten rooster living inside it? I'm not sure that you do. Even I don't want to go in there, so I think it's time to do something with that internal motivation I was talking about before.

After Mr Jameson takes the receipt from Folly, I reach into my own pocket. What you can't see from all the way down there is this piece of paper I have in there. But you have to set up the props ahead of time, or they won't be there when you need them. I take it out.

"I'm going to buy this," I say, giving Folly the paper.

He squints so he can read it. "I think you'd better get a different hairstyle if you're going to hustle people with a karaoke machine."

"I'm not hustling anyone," I say. "I want to buy it for the Juicebox. I bet Ruben could make money with this on the off-nights, when there's no show going on. No other place has karaoke in Hatahatchee. That's why Gram goes all the way to Tidewater Beach."

I went with her once when I was five and sang "Under the Sea". Gram used to sing in TV commercials, and she thought I'd like karaoke because I made a cardboard stage in the living room, and I was always singing and putting on shows, but it turned out that wasn't very good training for getting up in front of a live audience full of people I didn't know. I bet you've never seen knees shaking the way mine shook. Gram says I looked like an angel and I sounded like a waterlogged band saw. That's part of how I know that my real place is off to the side of the stage, not on it. Ruben knows it, too. Except for that time I had to fill in for CROWD MEMBER #1 in the parade scene in *James and the Giant Peach*, I keep myself well out of sight of the audience.

Mr Jameson takes the paper and says, "Aha. My old nemesis. Karaoke."

"What's a nemesis?" says Folly, who has never read a decent comic book in his life.

"It's an enemy," I say.

"Close," says Mr Jameson. "It means the thing that will bring you down in the end, and usually after you've been thinking too highly of yourself."

"So why is karaoke going to bring you down in the end?"

"Not *going* to bring me down. Brought me down." Then he sighs. "Boys, when you get married, marry someone who loves to sing." He stares off into the cosmos after he says that.

Folly says in that voice that makes women in the supermarket want to pet him, "May loves to sing, doesn't she, Sid? Remember how she sang that song with Mrs. Jameson at your mum's birthday that one time?"

That was in fourth grade, but you can bet Folly was on the love trail even then. I caught him hiding under the

Jamesons' window once, listening to Mrs Jameson giving May one of her voice lessons. Looking at him now, all suave and bow-tied, you wouldn't think he would do an undignified thing like that. But he did.

Mr Jameson just goes on, "But if that girl loves to sing, and she's got a voice like Billie Holiday, and you've got a voice like Elmer Fudd, don't enter a karaoke competition to try to win her heart. You might get the girl, but you'll never think about your singing voice the same way again. Before that competition, I was under the impression that I was a good singer. A very good singer. The trouble is, you can't tell a man he's lousy at something. You have to show him. And that karaoke machine showed me."

"So it brought down your singing career?" says Folly. Everything's a career with Folly, even if it's nothing but a hobby.

"Like the flimsy construction it was," says Mr Jameson. "Like a house of cards."

"Like the Tower of Babel," says Folly. He sits down in a chair next to Mr Jameson and stretches out like an old man watching cars go by. I won't be surprised if he shows up next Saturday wearing a fisherman's cap.

"So what's the plan, Sid?" asks Mr Jameson, waking himself up. "How does a nice kid like you pay for a machine like that? Do you have a secret money supply I don't know about? The wages of sin?"

"No, sir. I don't have any money supply." I don't want

him to think I'm complaining about not getting paid, though, so I say quickly, "But I'll figure out a way to earn it. There's lots of stuff I can do."

"That's right," Folly says. "And we have new product lines."

"What are your other lines?" Mr Jameson asks.

"Consumer goods," says Folly, like everyone knows what that means. "Useful household products. That kind of stuff."

"I'll be sure to let you know if I need anything," says Mr Jameson. He pulls the screen door open and wedges his chair part-way through. "Tell you what. Why don't I see how my tea's doing, and you two fat cats can discuss your business plan with the chickens."

"So, what is your business plan?" I ask as we go around to the back garden. I grab the rake and the work gloves from Mr Jameson's back porch.

"*Our* business plan, Sid." Now it's Folly's turn to show some internal motivation. He takes a sheet of paper out of his briefcase. "Have you ever heard of the Little Trixie Commerce Club?"

Pen has a subscription to *Little Trixie*. "You got this out of a little girl's magazine?" I told you Folly never read a good comic in his life.

Folly holds his head up high. "I didn't get it out of the magazine. I got it off the website. But look here." He shows me the paper, and I read what it says.

"I don't know if I want to join any Little Trixie club." I don't tell him that I can't believe Little Trixie is trying to con people into this kind of thing, when it's mostly five-year-old girls who read the magazine, anyway, and where are they going to get $9.99 or any other kind of money for investing in useful household goods?

"Too late. You're already in. I got a money order for one hundred and thirty-eight dollars and ninety-nine cents and sent it yesterday. That's everything I had from selling eggs plus sixty-seven cents I found in the car on the way to the post office."

"A money order? I didn't know you could order money." Maybe there's a website where I could order a stack of twenty-dollar bills at a discount. That would solve a lot of my problems.

"A money order," says Folly, like he can't believe he has to tell me this, "is like a cheque. You have to pay for it. It's safer than posting cash somewhere."

That's too bad for me, but I suppose if getting money was as easy as ordering it, nobody would have to work for anything.

Folly likes working. I can just see him walking into the post office with Frankie the Business Dog and strolling up to the counter like he runs all of Hatahatchee and halfway out into Bluewater Bay. Plonking down his $138.99 and smiling some kind of smile that fries Sherry the Post Office Lady's insides so she forgets to ask what a kid Folly's age is doing with money like that. Knowing Folly, he probably even tried to sell her some useful household goods on his way out of the door.

"So how am I part of it?" I ask. "I didn't put in any money." I hope he's not going to ask me to hand over half of $138.99, seeing as I can't get it out of a catalogue.

"No problem," he says. "I put you on the Board of Directors. You don't put in money, but you get to help decide how to spend our profits. Plus you get a nominal salary."

I don't know what nominal means, but since I've never had any salary before, it's an improvement. "What kind of household goods are we selling?"

"Useful ones. It's probably cleaning products. Maybe some vases and oven gloves and such. Kind of thing my mum would go crazy over. I bet they send us a catalogue or something, and we pick what we want to sell. At fifty per cent return, once you subtract the club membership fee, we could make–"

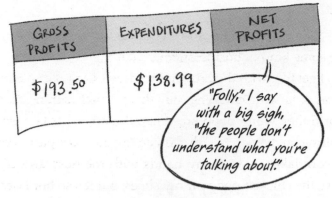

GROSS PROFITS	EXPENDITURES	NET PROFITS
$193.⁵⁰	$138.99	

"Folly," I say with a big sigh, "the people don't understand what you're talking about."

"I'm telling you, you've got to learn to LTN, Sid. Love the Numbers. We could make sixty-four dollars and fifty cents. And we just keep rolling all our profits back into the business until we're making some real money."

"And we're going to buy a karaoke machine for the Juicebox?"

"That'll be our charitable donation, to offset our taxes." He loses his business sense for a second and starts looking as soft and gloopy as a bowl of egg yolks. "May's a good singer, isn't she, Sid? I bet she'd use a karaoke machine."

I don't tell Folly that May scorns karaoke because she says she's a Real Singer, and real singers don't need the words up in front of them like senior citizens on a Tuesday night. I don't want to hurt his feelings.

Folly gets the eggs, all two dozen of them. The chickens like him better than they like me. They don't peck at his fingers when he goes in to take the eggs out, and they'll crouch down for him and let him hold their bony, feathery little selves. He heads off down the block with Frankie to cash in.

"See you at the Juicebox," I call as he goes, and he gives me some kind of businessman's salute.

I get to it with the rake and the fresh straw. I don't know what it is with chickens, but there is not a thing in this world they won't poop on. When I'm done, Mr Jameson is waiting on the porch with the iced tea and a couple of bowls of cornflakes. I wash my hands with the hose and try to rinse the chicken poop off my shoes, but it's so hot I decide to go barefoot, and I kick them off into the grass.

"Is there anything better than cornflakes on a Saturday morning?" he asks.

"Pink-sprinkle doughnuts are pretty good," I say, and Mr Jameson laughs.

"They are," he says. "I used to buy those down at Panhandle Pastries. Mrs Jameson could do some serious damage to a pink-sprinkle doughnut. But anyway, what's your question?"

It's got me down, thinking about Mrs Jameson so much. We only knew her for a couple of years, but she was May's favourite singing teacher, and even teeny-tiny Pen used to sit and dig in the dirt while she weeded the flowers.

I'm thinking about that picture again, and I want to help Mr Jameson find it. I know there's more useful stuff I could do for him, but finding that picture would make him the happiest. And when you're a director, you know that a big part of your job is making other people happy.

"Did you ever find that picture?" I ask.

"What picture is that?"

"The one you said was your favourite thing in the whole world."

I don't want to make him cry again. But he doesn't even sniffle. He just swivels and looks at me funny.

"You remembered that? Seriously? You've been thinking about that all this time? You are above average, Sidney. I wish I could tell you I had found it. But there are so many places in the house I can't get into so easily anymore."

"I could help you. I can get into all kinds of places." It's true. I am, like Gram says, just a quarter of a sliver of a kid. I can fit inside a chicken coop, after all. "But isn't the picture on your camera? Can't you print another one?"

Mr Jameson shakes his head. "Nope. Someone else took that picture, years ago, someone I can't get in touch with anymore. And I don't know if it was even taken on a digital camera. My friend just gave me the print. But you don't want to spend your summer crawling around my house when you could be at that theatre or jumping off the tyre swing down at Turkey Bayou, do you?"

The funny thing is, I do. I like to do things for people. "I can do all that, and help you, too. Besides, I'm always crawling around backstage finding props for the actors. You wouldn't believe how they lose stuff."

It's like that photo is a prop, and I have to make sure it's in Mr Jameson's hand when he needs it. "You're above average," Mr Jameson says again. "Hey, I have a question for you."

"You may ask me one question," I say, even though

36

he could ask me about a million questions and I'd answer every one.

He laughs. "What is it you like so much about that theatre?"

"The Juicebox?" I could go on about the Juicebox until Mr Jameson was sorry he ever asked me.

"Well, any theatre. Theatre in general. Mrs Jameson used to love any kind of performance, and I know your sister does." Mr and Mrs Jameson came to the Juicebox to see May in *A Little Princess* and again for a fairy-tale play where she was cast as about six different princesses. "But you like to hang out behind the scenes. Why is that?"

I think about that for a second. Of all the Juicebox kids, I'm the only one who prefers to be backstage. Like I said, I don't belong in the spotlight. But that doesn't mean what I do isn't important. The whole show depends on everything being set up the right way to start with – all the scenery, all the props, all the costumes. I help to make sure the play goes off without a hitch.

"Well," I say, "when I'm getting everything ready for a show, I feel just as excited as the kids going onstage. But I'm not focused just on my entrance, or my lines. I get to see the whole picture."

"That's a good way to look at things," says Mr Jameson. "Are you really worried the theatre is going to close down?"

"Not if I have anything to say about it." I try to sound more certain than I feel. "But we could use some luck."

And then suddenly I jump straight up out of my chair

and kind of slither onto the ground, and my ankle's on fire. I can see Mr Jameson trying not to laugh at me, which is probably a good skill for a Marine to have.

"It's good luck to get bitten by a fire ant," he says. "Trust me."

Act I

SCENE THREE

(It's a short one, so we're going back to the kitchen. It saves money to use the same sets and props over and over. That's how we do it at the Juicebox, too.)

I'd better get some more cast members out here. I wanted to do a whole first scene where I introduce everyone one by one, but Ruben told me once that people get bored easily and you have to keep things moving along. I don't want you to start yawning or anything, so you know what's the most exciting thing I can think of to put onstage?

A ghost.

Shh. Okay, here it comes.

The ghost enters stage right. It's wearing a dressing gown, and there's a chain around its neck, and it's sort of moaning like *Oooohhhhh-oooohhhh*. Usual ghost stuff.

The ghost opens its mouth like it's about to let out a good old blood-curdling scream, when it turns to look at me.

"*Aaaii* – oh, honeybunch, I didn't see you there."

"Hi, Mum."

Did you buy it? The whole ghost thing? It's okay if you didn't. Just don't tell Mum, because you'll hurt her feelings. She does make-up down at the Juicebox, and costumes and stuff, and any time she can fix it, she finds a part for herself as a ghost. I don't know why Ruben doesn't say no to ghosts in everything. I suppose it keeps things interesting. She's been one of the ghosts from *A Christmas Carol* and one of the ghosts from *Cinderella*. I know what you're thinking – that there are no ghosts in *Cinderella*. Well, there aren't until you've seen my mum being one.

Why ghosts all the time? Mum says a ghost in a play isn't too different from a mum in real life. It's there to remind you of your conscience.

"Are you practising something for the variety show?" I point at the chain.

"Just working on my technique. I was thinking maybe Ruben would want to do *The Canterville Ghost* in the autumn."

"So you think we're going to make enough money at the fundraiser tonight to have an autumn season?"

Mum puts her chain down and looks less like a ghost and more like a mum. "I hope so."

"I was thinking maybe if we had a karaoke machine, people would pay to come and sing there sometimes."

"Karaoke? Isn't that a bit loud? I don't know if Ruben wants that in the theatre. But we'll think of something,

Sid. The Juicebox means a lot to a lot of people. I've been volunteering there so long, I don't know what I'd feel like if it had to close down."

I know how I'd feel. Even though I have a dad and a mum, *and* there's a grandma coming in soon, I'd feel pretty much like an orphan.

There's just one more thing about this scene, before I forget.

Cue a sound effect: some paint cans knocking together, and maybe the sound of a ladder being put up against the side of a house. That's my dad. I don't want you to forget about him just because he's offstage working. Here's what he would be saying if he were here: "Work hard. Keep working. One day you'll get good." He's like the Zap Zapter of house painting.

You won't see him tonight, either, because he's doing the Moonlight Pet Adoption down at his other job at the Pet Palace. But he's not so far away that he won't make it here in time for his cue.

Let's see, we've got almost the whole family now, including a ghost. We've got chickens, a neighbour with a tragic past and a best friend who's got dollar signs in his eyeballs just like in the old cartoons. And there's May, riding her bike from one wing to the other just to be confusing. That's about it for setting the stage. When I'm a real director, I'm going to have a big budget for things like costumes and flashy lighting, but right now we're all just looking the way we always do. You could call this a rehearsal.

41

Act I

SCENE FOUR

(On the way to the Juicebox, and then at the Juicebox.)

May tried to hide all the meringues she made that morning because for some reason she doesn't want to sell them at the theatre, but Mum says we all have to do things we don't want to. I don't think I'm going to take the time to let you watch that argument, though. I have to make choices like that to keep things moving along. So when you see me get into the car with a tray of seventy-two meringues on my lap to sell at the concession stand, you just have to believe me that Mum won that round.

Gram sits up front so Mum can drop her off at Noni's Wigs on the way. Me and May and Pen and seventy-two meringues are crammed into the back while we drive into town.

"I think it's very nice of May to bake something to

support the theatre," says Gram. She must not be able to hear May grinding her teeth. "We all have to do our part."

"My *part*," May mutters just loud enough for us all to hear, "has lines and a solo, and I get to wear an amazing dress. That's my part. This is robbery."

Even Pen knows to ignore May when she's in that mood. When Gram gets out of the car, May bounces out of the back and into the front seat like she got shot out of a cannon.

I hand Gram one meringue on the sly when she comes to the back window to wish us luck.

She does a kind of half-wink. "Bless you, Sidney. And your hair looks terrific."

I smile. I know my hair looks terrific. I told you, I cut it myself.

The Juicebox is in a shopping centre, squeezed in between the Salvation Army and Country Time Market. It might not be the best part of town, but to me it shines like May's glittering eyelids. Ruben painted the sign on the front himself. It says *The Juicebox: A Children's Theatre* in big red letters. All the shows are for kids, and all the actors are kids, too. Except Mum.

You should see this theatre. Ruben built the stage himself from wood he got when they rebuilt the high school's theatre. It's got a trapdoor and everything, which is funny, because the stage is only two feet high. We haven't worked out when to use it yet, since even if you had a play where someone was supposed to fall into a pit of despair, this would only be a very shallow pit of despair. There's a lever at stage right, but I've never tried it. I don't even know if the door opens. But I do know that when I get old enough to be the director, I'm going to live right above the theatre like Ruben does.

There's a kind of hush that settles on me when I walk into the theatre, no matter how crazy everyone else gets. May heads straight to the dressing rooms, and Pen bounces up onto the stage and hides behind one of the thick black curtains. Me, I breathe in deep and take it all in, just like I'm seeing it for the first time. It's a small place with rows of folding chairs for the audience. We don't have a lot of lights or a really great sound system, but it's enough. It might not be as fancy as some huge Broadway theatre, but you know that feeling you get when you close your eyes for a second and you think anything could happen? Walking into the theatre, it's like I close my eyes and the whole world opens up.

Ruben's been the director at the Juicebox ever since May joined when she was seven years old. I can tell he's been busy today because his hair isn't stiff and shiny like when he's had time to put some gel in it. It's drooping into his eyes. He's kneeling on the floor in front of a girl I don't recognize. The girl has short brown hair, cut like she's playing Peter Pan. Mum tried to cut May's hair like that when she played Peter Pan, but May ran away and said she'd rather wear a wig. The girl is wearing an old yellow curtain, and the toes of a pair of work boots are sticking

45

out from underneath. I know the Juicebox has some money problems – that's what this whole fundraiser is about – but I don't think I've ever seen an actor wearing a curtain costume before.

"Sidney!" Ruben says through a whole mouthful of pins. "Are you ready for the biggest night of your life?"

Now, in a normal play, you have the biggest night of anyone's life come in way later, somewhere closer to the end. You don't start out that way, when you're still right at the beginning, otherwise everything that comes after is just a big let-down. But I don't correct him. Sometimes even the director of a play doesn't have total control over what's happening.

"I brought meringues for the concession stand."

Ruben shoots me a pin-faced grin. "I was hoping for more things to sell. It's like you answered my prayer."

He sticks a pin into a bunch of curtain at the girl's shoulder. "You know my cousin, Jelly Baby?" He nods at the girl, who moves her eyes over to me. She's a good actor, I think, because she knows she has to stand still or she'll get jabbed. She doesn't even risk a smile, but her eyes brighten up and seem to say hello. "Of course you don't know her. She lives in Miami. How could you know her? And she is named after a bag of sweets."

"What kind of sweets?" I ask.

"Jelly Babies, of course," says Ruben. He takes another pin and brings up a swoosh of curtain at Jelly Baby's waist.

"But you keep your giggles to yourself, okay? Jelly Baby is as tough as they come. Isn't that right?" He gives Jelly Baby a soft punch on the arm and lets go of all the fabric to see how it falls. "This is good, yeah? You can sew it up, Jelly Baby," Ruben says.

I want to ask why this girl called Jelly Baby's going to sew a costume when that's my mum's job, but Ruben goes off to help another kid with his lines. And before I can ask what the heck a Jelly Baby is, and if it's more like a jelly bean or a gummy worm, Jelly Baby goes through the door to the dressing room and disappears backstage.

The Juicebox is full of people today. Captain Hook (otherwise known as Brandon) is practising his swashbuckling with the sword. All the orphan kids from *Oliver!* are checking to make sure they look dirty enough. Everyone's running around with props or bringing pieces of their costume to Mum.

Ruben calls out to Captain Hook, "Careful with that sword, Brandon. If you break it, you will have to use the toilet plunger." Captain Hook's sword is the only one we've got, so it's also Long John Silver's sword, and it's the reason we've never done a production of *The Three Musketeers*. Long John Silver gets the sword first tonight, because when Captain Hook has it, it gets bent in half by the crocodile's jaws, and it takes some fixing to get it back into shape again.

This show tonight is not like a normal show. It's not just one play; it's bits and pieces of all kinds of plays we've done at the Juicebox. There's a flying scene and a sword-fighting scene from *Peter Pan* and that scene about painting fences from *Tom Sawyer*, and all kinds of other stuff, too. We have all the set pieces out at once, so we don't have to change things around for every different scene. So there's part of a pirate ship next to a balcony, and a picket fence and a backdrop of stars.

Ruben said if we don't raise enough money tonight for our next season, he's going to go back to painting boat bottoms in Jupiter. I said, "On Jupiter, you mean."

He said, "It's a town, you crazy kid."

I don't think Ruben would give up the good life at the Juicebox to paint boat bottoms in Jupiter or on Jupiter or anywhere else. And anyway, we're going to raise enough money for our next season and all the swords we want. I'm sure of it.

Time to help get things ready. I head for the stage, where Brandon's leaping backwards like the crocodile is about to snap his knees off. He lands on Tom Sawyer's fence. Jelly Baby comes out of the wings, still wearing the curtain. She helps Brandon up, and then she starts pulling the fence back into place.

"You'd better not be touching my balcony," calls a voice from the wings. "I need that for my performance." It sounds like something May would say, doesn't it? But it's not May. It's who May would be if she was still in the ten-to-twelve group: Beatrice, or like I used to call her, Beatrice the Swan, because she'll stretch her neck out three feet if it'll get her seen onstage. Now I call her Beatrice the Cockroach.

I mean, look at her. She's wearing a giant papier-mâché cockroach head.

It's because she picked a story called "Martina and Perez" for her part of folk tale week last spring, and that's what she's doing for the variety show, too. Martina is supposed to be a really beautiful cockroach that stands on a balcony and talks to all these animals that want to marry her. When I asked her if she realized she'd have to dress up like a cockroach in front of everyone, she just said, "But she's a *beautiful* cockroach." I suppose Beatrice would rather be a beautiful anything than her plain old self, even if it means having extra arms and antennae.

She was bragging for days about how her dad hired a professional architect to make that balcony for her, but it looks a little shaky to me. She made the cockroach head herself. It's sort of lumpy, and it sits on top of her head like a hood. She's painted long eyelashes and big red lips on herself, so you know without being told that even though she's a cockroach, she is a really beautiful lady.

Each of her cockroach legs has a paper bag on it. One of them is painted green and has big bulging eyes on it. That's supposed to be a frog. Beatrice said the others are a duck, a cat, a rooster, a cricket and a mouse, but they all look like paper bags to me. She made them so she could play all the parts herself. That's how she does things: her way or not at all. I never even bothered to tell her that with six fake legs plus her own two, she looks more like a spider.

She comes out and starts cooing – and that's not a word I use a lot, but it's the only kind of word for what she's doing. She makes a kissy face and coos, "Oh, Señor Frog," to the green paper bag. She asks each animal to make a noise, and all the animals frighten her except the mouse, whose name is Ratoncito Perez. They get married, and then he falls into a pot of soup and gets cooked to death. The End. The first time I heard it, I kept waiting for something else to happen: maybe Perez would come back to life, or it would turn out it wasn't him who fell into the pot after all, or some kind of twist to make everything turn out all right. But Ruben said some stories are like that. They just end, and things don't turn out all right. It sounded wise when he said it, but it doesn't make me feel good to think about it now.

"My grandma used to tell me that story," says Jelly Baby. "She learned it in Cuba when she was a kid. I can help you practise if you want."

"I don't *practise*," Beatrice squeals. "I *rehearse*, and I don't need *your* help to do that. All I need is my six legs."

"You only have five," says Jelly Baby. "Or seven, depending on how you count them."

It's true. Beatrice is missing a leg – the one that's supposed to have the cricket on it.

She swings around and gives Jelly Baby a look that is all cockroach and not one bit beautiful. "Well, where is it?"

50

"Do you want me to help you make a new one?" says Jelly Baby, and I suppose she doesn't see how close Beatrice is to spitting cockroach juice all over her. "I have to fix my puppets all the time. I swear they go out and get into trouble when I'm not looking. My great-grandfather used to say they had minds of their own."

"This isn't a puppet, it's my costume! Besides, who ever saw a puppet this big?"

"Well, I–" Jelly Baby starts to say, but Beatrice cuts her off.

"Besides, you should never wear yellow in the theatre. It's bad luck." She looks Jelly Baby over and throws her head to one side. Her antennae bobble up and down, and one of them comes loose.

"It's always been good luck for me," says Jelly Baby.

"You should take that thing off. It looks stupid, anyway."

Jelly Baby doesn't do what any one of the Juiceboxers would do, which is sing, "Baby Bea, Baby Bea, brain no bigger than a flea", and then watch Beatrice crack open and spew like a volcano. It's not even the flea part that gets her. It's the Bea part. "Be-a-trice!" she shouted the first time someone called her Baby Bea. "My name is *Be-a-trice*!"

Jelly Baby just says, "Do you want some help fixing that antenna, too?"

Now Beatrice is shaking so much, she might lose another leg or two. "You think you can show up and take over the ten-to-twelves just because you're Ruben's cousin and you have a weird name?" she practically shouts.

"I have a great name," says Jelly Baby, and she does a little twirl in her curtain. It seems that's too much for Beatrice to take, because she puts a foot down on the edge of the curtain dress almost like it's an accident. The pins come loose, and all Ruben's careful work is messed up. Jelly Baby grabs the curtain before it falls to the floor and holds it carefully. She starts pulling the pins out and putting them one by one in her shirt pocket.

Beatrice doesn't stop there. "Anyway, aren't your parents gone or something, and that's why you're here for the summer? What are you, an orphan?"

Beatrice starts walking away, and Jelly Baby's eyes track her like follow spots. Instead of lighting Beatrice for a solo, though, it looks like Jelly Baby wants to burn a hole right through her. But she doesn't say anything, she just goes backstage, and that's how you know that even though Jelly Baby goes around wearing curtains, she's a class act.

"She's just trouble," says Beatrice after Jelly Baby's gone. She's trying to get her antennae to sit right. "You know she does some stupid puppet act? Ruben wants her to do it here, but I hope she never does. We're not a little kids' puppet theatre, right?"

"What's the difference between a puppet and that paper-bag mouse you made?"

Beatrice looks flustered for a second. "I'm an *actor*," she says, and then like she's not one bit mad anymore, she says, "Oh, Sid, will you get my hand mirror for me?" That's because she knows she can't be angry with me forever if she wants her props set out right.

I say, "Aw, you don't need any help, Bea," and I hop down off the stage.

Jelly Baby's gone up to Ruben's apartment, which is a no-go zone for all us kids who aren't his cousin.

I don't think she's trouble. I think she's great. I'm trying to picture her doing a puppet show at the Juicebox. Is she going to put a tiny little theatre in the middle of the big stage and hide behind it, and make all kinds of funny voices? And why does Ruben think that's going to have anything to do with saving this theatre?

But I don't question Ruben. I go and find Folly instead. The concession stand is just a table with snacks and drinks that Folly sets up at the back of the theatre, but he's been running it like it's in a football stadium since I started managing all the props two summers ago. You don't sneak a cookie from Folly's concession stand without getting a lecture on shrinkage, which is his way of saying stealing.

At first, Ruben wasn't sure he should give all that responsibility to a kid, but Folly has a way of making you see past the kid on the outside to the gold-plated ledger book that lurks inside him. It didn't take long for Ruben to see it was a wise move to bring Folly on board. You've never seen so many ladies buy the lumpy old cookies and green Rice Krispies squares that all the Juicebox kids bring in to sell. Folly went one better, too: he went over to Panhandle

Pastries and asked Miss Alabama Harper to donate cookies, and seeing that she's an old Juicebox star herself and Folly can sell sharks to the ocean, she said yes.

All the food is set out neatly on plastic trays, and Folly's passing time reading a book called *You + Everyone = Sales: 101 Strategies for Getting Your Customers to Say YES!* Zap Zapter must be immortal because the picture on the back of all his books is the same. Same smile, same suit jacket and same shiny gold bow tie.

Ruben stops by the concession stand. "Hey, Folly, is Miss Francolina ready for her time in the sun?" Frankie lifts her head up when she hears her name, and even though she's a dog, I swear she gives out a little purr. It was Ruben who picked Frankie's name, after this Spanish nursery rhyme that goes *Francolina the hen laid an egg in the kitchen* (I mean, it says all that in Spanish). Only in real life, it was something else Frankie laid, and it was on the stage, not in the kitchen, but you get the idea.

You can't get Folly onstage for anything, but Frankie's a different story. She's a spotlight-hog dog, every bit as desperate as Beatrice to get noticed. Tonight she's playing Argos, the faithful dog of Odysseus (played by Noah), who was trying to get home after a big war but instead spent ten years sailing around getting himself lost. Argos waits for him on a big pile of manure – hey, don't look at me, that's how the story goes. When Odysseus finally gets home, and he's dressed up like a beggar so no one will recognize him,

Argos still knows who he is, because that's what dogs do. Odysseus says hi to Argos and scratches him behind the ears, and then Argos just dies. I suppose he thought he'd done enough waiting around. Frankie has been practising her falling-down-dead moves, and she's just about perfect.

"She is," says Folly. He scratches Frankie behind the ears and she drops to the ground and rolls onto her back, legs all everywhere and tail beating out the last three thumps of her heart. Ruben claps. Frankie jumps up, because clapping is her cue, and she bows her head. It's going to bring the house down.

"I've been doing some calculating," Folly goes on, "and I think we could increase our profits by offering the customer a combo deal with a cookie and a drink together. See, the drink mix only costs eleven cents per cup, and if you charge–"

"Fine," says Ruben with a grin. He knows Folly too well to want to let him get started talking like a calculator. "You are the businessman. Make up a sign." He reaches for a meringue, and Folly and Frankie both move in on him fast. Folly slides the tray away, because he wants to make as many sales as he can, and I know it's also because these are *May's* meringues and he's a gallant type of gentleman, at least in his own mind. Frankie snaps at Ruben's leg because she's devoted to Folly, and if Folly is devoted to May, then so is she. Ruben holds up his hands. "Okay, okay. I should know better than to mess with you."

After Ruben leaves, Folly goes to wash his hands and then starts making the drinks up in a plastic jug.

I'm filling the jug with water. "You really think we're going to make enough money selling household products to buy that karaoke machine for the Juicebox?"

Folly gives one quick, sure nod. "They're useful, I keep saying. We're going to make a boatload. Look here."

He grabs a napkin and draws a little graph:

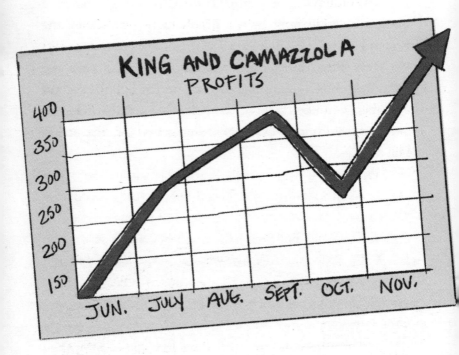

"I'm projecting over the next six months. See, we're going to increase our profits pretty steadily, and of course we'll re-invest some of the money into the business, but starting around September, we're going to have a setback. You always have a setback, so we might as well just plan for it. But when people start their Christmas shopping, you know what they want to buy for their grannies?"

"Useful household products?"

"Absolutely."

I'm noticing how Folly's graph looks like something Ruben showed us once, about how a play goes. You start out with rising action in the first act, when you work out what the problem is, and it keeps rising through the second act when you keep having more problems, but when you get to the third act, and everything gets fixed, the action falls.

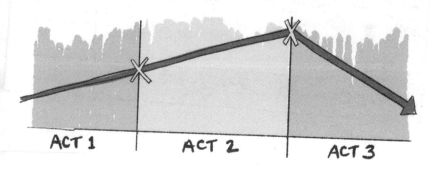

Only Folly's an optimist, so his graph's got some more rising action at the end.

Those Xs are where there's a catastrophe, which is just a way of saying there's a sudden change in events. Catastrophe is the soul of the theatre. That's what Ruben says, and he's never wrong.

"The only thing we have to worry about," says Folly, nudging the front row of cookies into place, "is getting above ourselves once we get all that money. Zap says he who gets above himself can't ever rise to the heights."

I'm thinking this over when Jelly Baby finds us, and she's got that yellow curtain over her arm now. "Don't worry about Beatrice," I say, because I want Jelly Baby to know we're not all like that here.

She says, "If I'm worried about anything, it's not Beatrice," and then she asks just about the worst question I've ever been asked. "Sid, can I pin this on you?" Jelly Baby holds up the curtain. "Ruben said you wouldn't mind."

I try to dodge her, but I trip. You try getting away from a girl who wants to wrap you up in a curtain. You might trip over your shoelaces, too.

From the floor, I say, "But isn't that your costume? It'll be the wrong size if you fit it to me."

"It's not my costume," says Jelly Baby, hauling me up and starting with the pins faster than I can make any sense of. "It's for Doña Flor Amarilla."

Folly has the kindness not to laugh at me, but his pose

says, *I am not affiliated with these people, and this is exactly why I only run the concession stand.*

"Who's–" I start to say, but I can't get the name out fast enough. Jelly Baby sticks the last pin, and then Ruben calls beginners to their places so we can run through the show one last time. Even though I'm the director of this little show I'm telling you about, he's the director of the variety show, and so I go to where I'm supposed to be backstage, ready to hand out props, dressed like some kind of second-rate banana.

Act I

SCENE FIVE

Wait, hang on a second.

I think I'll make that cast list now. That's a real theatre thing. It's how you keep everything straight when you're writing a play, and it's how the audience keeps it straight, too. I should have done it at the start, but people keep showing up in the middle of things. Here's what the cast list looks like:

CAST OF CHARACTERS

SIDNEY HORATIO CAMAZZOLA...................me, and I'm only first because I entered the scene first. That's how it works.

FOLLY KING...................Sid's best friend, future millionaire and BMW owner

FRANCOLINA...................Folly's dog, Argos, shoe thief (but you haven't seen that part yet)

MAY............big sister, crazy about egg whites and sometimes just plain crazy

PENELOPE...............little sister, half pirate and all pain in the neck

MR JAMESON.............................neighbour and employer

DAD.............................house painter and noise maker

MUM.............................ghost pirate, ruling hand

GRAM.............................karaoke superstar

RUBEN............manager and director of the Juicebox Theatre, Hatahatchee's one and only home for theatrical kids

JELLY BABY.......................new girl, mystery puppeteer

BEATRICE..................Beatrice the Swan, Beatrice the Cockroach

Those are the big parts. There are some bit players, too, like Noah and Brandon and all the other Juicebox kids. And there's Miss Alabama Harper and Folly's mum and good old Zap Zapter, but they're just names so far. Oh, I suppose I should have put them on the cast list. But you know who they are now.

Sometimes you can save on actors and have one person play more than one part, if the parts aren't ones with a lot of lines and they're not in the same scenes. Don't worry, though. I'm not going to get things criss-crossed by having people play different parts here. Pen is Pen and Folly is Folly, and you don't have to imagine one of them dressed up like the other and wearing a wig. Well, Folly wouldn't wear a wig. Maybe some of the others would.

* * *

So. That's it so far.

Makes it easier to know who you're dealing with, doesn't it? I know I feel better.

If you're feeling overwhelmed, don't worry. Halfway through, you get to take a break. It's called intermission. But we're not there yet.

Act I

SCENE FIVE

for real

(Still at the Juicebox. But this time the house lights are down and we're all business, about to start the variety show.)

I can see from where I am that the house isn't half as full as we wanted it to be. But Ruben acts like it's just fine. He acts, you see, because this is the theatre. And I act, too, even though I already told you I'm no good at it.

I'm backstage, waiting to hand out props and generally make sure we're operating smoothly. But first, Ruben has to welcome everyone like he always does, in his black silk director's shirt. Black is a special colour in the theatre because it doesn't reflect light. That's why the stage and the curtains and everything are black, and Ruben's shirt is black, like he's just another part of the scenery. The only things shining are his hair, because he's put some gel in it, and his face, because he's nervous about tonight. Me, too.

Ruben gives a fine speech. It seems like the audience wants to make up for being small by being loud. I hope they also try to make up for it by being extra hungry at intermission.

The show starts off pretty well. First comes part of *Treasure Island*, where Mum/the ghost of Long John Silver goes on to have a swordfight with the cabin boy, Jim Hawkins, who's armed with a stick I found backstage, then out comes Tom Sawyer, and then Captain Hook and Peter Pan. Good. Everyone's got the right props and I haven't confused any of the different plays. Then, of all people, Eponine from *Les Miserables* comes out to sing that song she sings that makes everyone cry. I tried to tell her that *Les Mis* is not a kids' play and we don't do it at the Juicebox, but Eponine told me to go and make friends with an alligator.

You've already met Eponine, by the way. That's May.

May can sing the heck out of any song, though, so the audience gulps it down. She's amazing. I said it. All Mum's and Grandma's stage talent went to her, plus whatever genius rubbed off on her from those voice lessons she had with Mrs Jameson.

Frankie's big moment is coming up. She takes her place by the cockroach balcony, and I think she's pretending that she's on a big pile of manure. I tried to get Ruben to build some stage manure, but he said he wanted the audience to use their imagination for that.

Along comes Odysseus, stumbling and dragging himself across the stage, and you should see Frankie. She's in her element. She raises her head just a little and lets Odysseus rub her muzzle and scratch behind her ears. All the while, he's doing his soliloquy, which is a theatre way of saying he's talking to himself, and Frankie is drinking the whole thing in like it's someone else's milkshake. When Odysseus starts stumbling away, Frankie lets her tongue roll out and falls to the floor just like she's a real dead dog, and the small audience goes crazy, clapping and whistling and stomping their feet.

This is more than Frankie can take, it seems, because she gets up on cue but she doesn't bow. She kind of skittles around backwards and barks and knocks into Odysseus, who's hanging out by the doorway in the balcony set waiting to say his final line. The audience laughs, but it's nervous laughter, like they don't know if this is part of the scene or not.

Odysseus loses his balance and falls into the set, and the set rocks back and forth because it looks like the professional architect Beatrice's dad hired does not know how to build for the theatre. Finally it teeters over enough that Frankie scrabbles around making that awful toenails-on-the-floor sound, although I don't know if the audience can hear that over the sound of falling set pieces. Frankie hightails it offstage, directly into the audience, before the set crashes down, trapping the trailing end of Odysseus's raggedy robes underneath and yanking them off his body. Odysseus is left standing there under the lights in nothing but his SpongeBob boxer shorts.

I couldn't have directed that any better.

Now the audience is making all kinds of noises, everything from kids squealing that there's a dog running around to grown-ups trying to shush their kids, to chairs getting knocked over in all the excitement.

Because I take care of all the props, I feel I should also take care of any actors who freeze up onstage like coat racks. I whisper from backstage, "Noah! Scene over! Make your exit!"

I'm betting Odysseus never knew what it felt like to have the world see you in nothing but your cartoon underpants. Noah does a stiff bow and backs offstage, but not before he almost catches it again, this time from Beatrice, who's got her whole pretty-cockroach costume on because she was supposed to go on next.

"That dog!" shrieks Beatrice, running onstage. "That dog destroyed my set! You're going to owe me a lot of money for this," she yells at Frankie, who's sitting in a corner licking away all her embarrassment.

It seems like the audience has calmed down, now that Frankie's staying still and the chairs have been put back in place. People are settling back in, and maybe it's just possible that they think this was all planned out. They can keep on thinking that.

Ruben's up on the stage now, and he guides Beatrice backstage. She's howling, "It's all ruined, it's ruined," and he's trying to get her to sit down and take off her cockroach headpiece because her tears are getting the papier-mâché all soggy. She refuses to do her piece without her set, even though Ruben swears it would be just as good if she was standing on the stage instead of up on her balcony.

Beatrice's nose is right up on Ruben's silk shirt, and something that looks like tiny silver snakes is coming out all over the place. Ruben looks at me the way a person does when he's got life-size cockroach snot dripping down his front. That look says, *Do something, Sid. Anything.*

We've got five minutes to fill before the curtain was supposed to come down. We could end early, but I'm a big believer in giving people their money's worth. No one else is prepared to go out. Most of the kids are already out of their costumes, and Noah is still sitting at a dressing table in his SpongeBob boxers like he thinks all the clothes in the world won't cover up his shame.

Ruben says that sometimes in the theatre you have to do things upside-down. Not like you're hanging from your knees on a trapeze, but like you're doing the opposite of what people expect. So that's why I'm onstage, fidgeting under the lights, instead of backstage where nature intended me to be.

I open my mouth. Then I close it. This is bad. This is worse than when Pen ate all the props for *Charlie and the Chocolate Factory* and chewed them ten times each, and they weren't even supposed to be edible. This is worse than when a normal actor goes out and forgets their lines, because I don't have lines. There's no one in the wings whispering my prompts.

The only thing I can think of, the only thing that catches any light down there in the deep dark part of my brain that remembers what to do when the jaws of death are closing in, is singing. Singing like I'm five years old and Gram has cajoled me into getting on the stage at the Pick n' Play. How does "Under the Sea" start, now? I open my mouth again and suck in a breath like I'm trying to hold the whole Juicebox together in my lungs. It's going to be the saddest *a cappella* calypso performance in the history of Florida. I am overheating with shame. You couldn't cool my cheeks down now if you threw a chunk of dry ice at me. I'd rather be caught in the spotlight wearing SpongeBob boxers. I'd rather–

I'm still wearing that curtain. I didn't know it before, but I know it now. I can feel every yellow inch of it. I must look like a costume mannequin, which is what I suppose I am, but I feel huge, like the Statue of Liberty gone wrong. The Statue of Liberty, if she didn't get her robes back from the dry cleaner in time to go and stand in the harbour. I'd go and hide in the corner with Frankie, just curl up like an armadillo until the house was empty, but I'd have to get closer to the audience to do that, and besides, I can't even leave the stage. Me and the spotlight are one, and as long as it's shining, I'm standing and staring, until something comes along to rescue me. I could be up here all night. All I can say is, I'm glad I can't see the faces in the audience, because I don't want to know what they think of me or my curtain.

And then I hear music. I don't recognize it, but it sounds like the music Ruben plays during our Walk This Way warm-ups, when we hop, slither or otherwise get ourselves across the stage according to what we think the music is asking us to do. Right now, it's some kind of Cuban jazz or I don't know what. And I hear feet tapping along. I unstick myself enough to see what's coming from backstage, and it's a good thing I'm not putting this all down in a real script because I have no idea what I'm seeing.

It's some kind of walking doll. It's huge, is all I can say. Huge and yellow. I'm ashamed to say we could be twins in our yellow dresses, except the giant doll's dress has a rip down the front. It's got a giant old lady's head and wobbly arms held up by sticks. It comes right up to me, and I don't run because, like Folly and Zap Zapter say, you can only rise to the occasion if you're there for it.

But the giant doll gives me a little bump with its shoulder, which I take to be my cue to exit, and I don't need telling twice.

When I get to the safety of the wings, I start pulling that curtain off, but I still keep an eye on the stage because I've got to know what that doll's planning to do next. It – she? – is kind of swaying to the music, and she starts kicking her feet up in time, faster and faster as the music speeds up.

Ruben's standing behind me in a black T-shirt. I suppose Beatrice finally let him go, but her cockroach slime ruined his black silk director's shirt. Maybe one piece of equipment a director needs is a good-size handkerchief or a bib or something. He nods along with the beat and whispers, "She's good, isn't she?" And then I see that the feet walking that doll around are wearing work boots.

"That's Jelly Baby?" I whisper back. "*That's* a puppet?" Pen never had anything like that in her puppet basket at nursery.

"*That* is Doña Flor Amarilla."

There's that name again. This play is full of characters who just wrote themselves into the script, but I don't ask why. I zip a lip and just watch. After she finishes her dance, Jelly Baby sways up to the front of the stage and starts talking.

"Había una vez, once upon a time in the old city of Habana . . ."

She's telling Beatrice's story, the one about the beautiful cockroach. If Beatrice wasn't three shades of purple before, she will be now. It's Jelly Baby's first night at the Juicebox, and she's upstaging grumpy old Bea. She goes on to describe the balcony that used to be there, that is now in halves behind her, and makes it sound like it was some kind of palace. I wait for Beatrice to tear out there and throttle her.

But Jelly Baby does something funny. When she describes Martina the cockroach, she turns her enormous head towards where Beatrice is standing in the wings, all droopy and furious, and she waits.

"Beatrice," whispers Ruben, "you go on now. She is setting the stage for you."

"She stole my story!" Beatrice snaps. "I'm not going out there. I'm not some bit player in her puppet show."

"She is only trying to make up for your balcony. She wants to help."

Beatrice won't even answer. She goes purpler and stalks off, which I know is the right way to say it because her legs look as stiff as a couple of celery stalks. Ruben shrugs and waves to Jelly Baby to keep going.

I have my loyalty to the Juicebox, and I guess that means I have my loyalty to the kids who have been there for years like Beatrice has, but the way Jelly Baby tells that story, it's like I never heard it before. There's none of that cooing and prancing that Beatrice does, just Jelly Baby's voice, which is now Doña Flor Amarilla's voice, carrying all the way to the back of the house as smoothly as a boat sliding through bayou water. And that's the only thing you hear until she's done, and the whole house rocks with clapping. She doesn't take the puppet off her head when she's done, though. She backs up slowly, twisting and bowing until she's offstage.

I want to tell her that that puppet is incredible. It looks like it knows about everything there is to know about a person. It's like how Gram would look, if Gram was a puppet. But I'm shy for some reason, and besides, I don't know if she can hear me while it's still on her head.

Ruben helps lift the giant puppet up over her, and that little waif May goes out to thank the audience for coming and leads all the bowing, holding her hand out as Juiceboxers come out from the wings in pairs.

Someone else gets back onstage to bow, too, now that there's clapping going on: Frankie, like she never caused a theatre catastrophe in her life. I don't go out to bow, because the stage crew doesn't bow, but even if we did I think I'd keep myself under wraps this time. I've had enough sweating under the lights to last me a good long while.

This would be the place to end the scene, except there's one thing you probably want to know about, and Folly would agree with you: did we make enough money to keep the Juicebox boat afloat?

Once the house is empty, I go to check in with Folly at the concession stand.

"How'd we do?"

Folly has the honour of counting up all the dollars and piles of change. He spreads them out, counts them and stacks them, and spreads them out again, like he thinks maybe he got it wrong the first time.

"Not as good as we would have done if Frankie hadn't eaten all those meringues," he grumbles. Except Folly never grumbles. He's too sunny for that.

"She did?" I can imagine Frankie eating all kinds of things that she shouldn't eat, even things that aren't food, but I would never have guessed she'd eat meringues.

"Well, she must've. I had to make a gentleman's call right after she ran offstage, and when I got back, they were all gone."

"Was there dog slobber on the tray?" Frankie is known far and wide for her ability to spread drool.

"Tray was gone, too."

"Then it wasn't her. See? If Frankie took them, the tray would be on the ground. If the whole tray disappeared, it had to have been a person. Maybe we have a meringue thief on our hands."

This makes Folly brighten up. Frankie may be a vandal, but he wouldn't like to think of her as a thief, too. "I think you're on to something. Anyway, we only have forty-six dollars here. That won't keep the lights on for a month."

Who's going to steal meringues from a kids' theatre concession stand? What kind of low-down somebody does that?

On my way to the box office, which is really just a folding table by the door, I bump into May, who's staggering under the weight of a pile of costumes. She must be taking them home for Mum to mend.

"Watch it, Sid," she says, and hustles out the door. She must be in a terrible mood, because normally she can think of a dozen more creative things to call me than my own name.

Ruben and Mum are counting money out on the table, and I just catch Mum shaking her head. Folly and Frankie come over to join us. Folly puts the concession stand money on the table next to the ticket money.

"Not good enough?" I ask, because you might as well stare truth squarely in the face. If Zap Zapter doesn't already say that, he probably should.

"Nope," Mum says softly. "Not this time."

I look at Ruben. "Are you going back to Jupiter?" I'm scared he'll say yes. Maybe even his very own karaoke machine wouldn't get him to stay now.

He just taps the counter with his fingernails. "We'll see," he says.

That's about the scariest answer I can think of.

Mum's looking at Ruben, Ruben's looking at Folly, and Folly's looking down at the pitiful money. Mum puts her hand on my shoulder. Ruben looks like he wants to move but he can't decide where to go.

Whenever there's a moment like that in a good play, you have a couple of possibilities. Either there's going to be a sad song – and trust me, there's not going to be any song here – or something comes along to bust up the atmosphere and make anyone who's feeling bad feel worse. Because this is a really good play, you can guess who comes out to ruin everything.

Beatrice must be looking for something else to wipe her nose on, because it's still red and runny and it makes her look like an angry toddler. "That balcony cost money, you know, and since it was *your* dog, I'm going to take it out of *your* hide, Sidney Camazzola. He's a menace, and he ought to be put down."

I'm not going to argue about whose dog Frankie is, or if she's a boy dog or a girl. I only know I don't yet have any money hiding anywhere, so good luck to her trying to get at it. "Hey," I say, because I hate to watch cockroaches cry, "I bet if you'd got up on that balcony it would've fallen over anyway, and you'd have crushed all your antennae and legs and everything. Lucky for you, Frankie got there first."

"I wish he'd got himself crushed," is all Beatrice says, mean kid that she is. "Didn't I say there shouldn't ever be dogs or yellow costumes in the theatre? And don't get me started on puppets, or whatever that thing is. I thought this was a real theatre, for real actors, not some kind of little kids' morning TV show. Why does she have to wear that thing on her head? Puppets go on your hands, not your head."

Who's Beatrice to talk about someone wearing something on their head?

Like she heard me thinking this, she adds, "Mine's a costume. Costumes are different."

"On the bright side," says Mum, "now there's another girl in your age group, Beatrice, at least for the summer. Won't that be nice after all this time?"

That must be Mum's conscience-guard doing its job, trying to nudge Beatrice into saying something nice for once. Doesn't work, though.

"I was doing just fine before she came along."

"It takes a lot of skill to manipulate a puppet like Doña Flor," Ruben says. "Our great-grandfather brought her from Cuba when he was doing a special tour with his own children's theatre troupe. Now Doña Flor belongs to Juliana, and she performs with a theatre in Miami. You should ask her about it sometime."

Beatrice sends a stream of angry air out through her nose. "Like I'm going to do that. That puppet doesn't even look like a real person. Who would believe that that thing could move around on its own when it's sitting on top of her like that?"

"It's not always important to make the audience believe that something is real. Sometimes we have to show them what is not real," Ruben says gently. "Do you think the audience will truly believe that you are a cockroach?"

It doesn't even take antennae to make me believe it.

ACTORS' NOTES

It's part of a director's job to give notes to the actors to tell them what's good about their performance and what maybe isn't so good about it. When Ruben gives notes, he never writes them down because he doesn't want some kid to feel like they just got handed a report card. He just says quietly to everyone, one by one, what their strengths are and where they need a little improvement.

I'm going to have to write this down, because Beatrice ran off, and I went home anyway. The thing about Beatrice's performance is that it always comes right from the gut. You have no problem seeing if she's really mad or really happy or what, because it's all right there. That can be good and bad. My advice for her is that she has to work out how to show the quiet end of her range. She's really good at showing the loud end.

I would give her another note, too, but it's not about her performance. It's about her motivation. We're a group here at the Juicebox, and even though everyone has their own motivation, we have one goal: we have to keep this place going. I need this theatre, and I know Beatrice needs it, too, even though sometimes she acts like she's too big for us. So she has to find a way to be a part of this team and not just one lone cockroach who's in it for herself.

I bet Folly has some great saying from Zap Zapter about teamwork. Maybe I'll ask him. I know what Ruben says, though. He says, "The theatre is like life, only better."

See if old Zap can beat that.

Act II

SCENE ONE

(We're back on Hatahatchee Street. I'm in my back garden, thinking about chickens and theatres, and if I'm out here by myself too long I'm going to start thinking about some kind of chicken theatre.

When you get to a new act, you ought to start off with a bang. Sometimes it's funny and sometimes it's just unexpected. I went with funny. I'd put a thunderstorm in, too, but that's more of an Act III thing. So it's just hot again and clouds are hanging right above your head and your clothes feel like they're made of duct tape, the way they stick to you. The difference between this hot day and the last hot day you read about is that this one starts with a chase sequence.)

Gram comes running out of the house and into the back garden. She's hobbling because she's just got one shoe on, but for a grandma, she's making pretty good time. Frankie outpaces her, though, because Frankie has four feet and no conscience to weigh her down. She's off into the woods before Gram can get halfway across the garden.

"Sid! Oh, Sid, Francolina's bitten off one of my shoes and dragged it into the woods. I need that shoe, darling. Be a good boy and get it for me."

Gram limps to a stop, looking like someone who would consider kicking a dog with her other orange high-heeled shoe if she got within kicking distance. "Your daddy was going to drop me down at the Pick n' Play in half an hour, and I have to have that shoe." Which means I have to stop daydreaming and get in motion.

The woods go all along behind our house, so big and green and deep that you would never see the snakes until they were crawling up your leg. Mr Jameson says there are bears, too. I've never seen a bear in there, but once I saw Francolina run out like she swallowed a mouthful of mosquitoes and she wouldn't go back in for a week.

Gram waves her hand. "Hurry, Sid, or that shoe'll never see daylight again."

I take off running, but I catch my foot on the hose and kind of throw myself forwards, hoping if I leap far enough I won't fall on my face. Or into one of Pen's bear traps. When Folly told her there might be a bear in the woods, she took every sharp thing she could find and hid it in the grass. Folly doesn't have any little sisters, so he doesn't know that you can't go telling them things like that. I picked up a lot of scissors and the insides of our blender, but I'm glad the mower's broken because I bet there's still something hiding out there and I don't want to find it like that.

I miss the bear traps, but I stumble over a shovel, and

I swear that once I'm done here, I'm going to cut Pen's eye patch into tiny pieces and make her forget about being a pirate ever again. But this is no time for revenge. Gram's counting on me.

I cut across Mr Jameson's garden. There aren't any fences between gardens on Hatahatchee Street. Some people don't like that, but it makes for good running.

At the edge of the woods, I stop and listen in case Frankie's fast little feet are trotting where I can hear them. I do hear something – some set of feet crunching through the pine needles and oak leaves.

"No bears in here!" someone shouts.

I catch a glimpse of orange, but it's too bright to be Frankie. It's May coming out along the footpath, wearing Dad's orange Gators hat. May is all kinds of places today that I don't expect her to be. I saw her riding her bike towards town again this morning, and today wasn't an egg day. Come to think of it, I never even saw her whipping her egg whites, so who knows what she was doing.

"Hey, May, have you found Frankie yet?"

"I did not come out on this ugly old afternoon looking for that ugly old dog. That's your business, not mine. Why? What're you looking for her for?"

"She's got Grandma's shoe."

May tilts her head. "Which one?"

"One of the orange ones."

"Good. I never did like those."

"Why're you saying there are no bears in the woods?"

She pulls the cap down on her head. "Well, there aren't, are there?"

She strolls off, only it's faster than strolling. It's more like avoiding. Like there's something she doesn't want me to know.

Why May, who is disgusted not just by snakes, but by bugs and grass and dandelions, would come out for a walk in the woods is a mystery to me. But I don't have time to worry about her. I have to get Gram's shoe. I find the start of a narrow trail and go into the woods, saying the anti-snake prayer Folly and I made up two summers ago: *Dear God, don't let a snake bite me, oh Lord, do not let a snake bite me in the leg.*

It seems to work, because no snakes bite me. And there up the way a little is crazy old Francolina, lying on the pathway chewing delicately on one of Gram's second-favourite singing shoes like she was born to do it. You wouldn't think a dog would really go and steal a shoe straight off someone's foot, but I have seen stranger things.

"Gimme that, Frankie," I tell her. "I thought dogs only chewed shoes in cartoons. Drop it. *Drop it.*"

She looks up at me, chews for a second and then drops the shoe, probably thinking she doesn't want it anymore anyway. It's lost its taste. But when I pick it up, I see it's gained a few tooth marks on the heel.

Frankie follows me back to Folly's garden, on the other

side of Mr Jameson's house. I clip her to the long lead that's tied around a skinny tree trunk and give her head a good scratching. Right on cue, she flops down.

It's not her fault we have no fences, and it's not her fault a dog's got to be free. I give her one last sniff of the shoe, and she looks at me with the face of a condemned woman. I can see she got a taste for the dramatic playing Argos. "Sorry, girl," I say. "Not this time."

I say sorry to Gram, too, as I hand her one mangled orange high-heeled shoe.

"You think Cinderella ever had to put up with this?" she asks, wiping the dog slobber off her shoe and stuffing her foot into it.

"You're not a dog person, are you, Gram?" I ask.

She shakes her head. "But I am a grandson person, and that's even better. Now, would you go inside and fetch my curlicue for me? I'm about ready to go, and you know I need my curlicue."

Gram isn't bald anymore, but that doesn't stop her from wearing wigs just for fun. She says she got into the habit when she was going through chemotherapy for her cancer four years ago, and since that was the best part of the whole thing, she kept it up. So now she might show up at karaoke night with different kinds of hair, maybe a different colour or all swooshed up in a clip – that's what her curlicue looks like. I know just where that curly fountain of fake hair is – on the dressing table in her room – and I run in for it. Gram's such a pro with that thing, she doesn't even need to look in a mirror to get it straight on her head.

When I get back outside, I tell her all about my plan to buy a karaoke machine for the Juicebox so we can make money on the off nights.

"Oh, Sid," she says, fixing up the curlicue, "you don't make money off the karaoke machine." She lowers her voice. "You make money off the drinks, and the kind of drinks that make the most money are the ones you can't sell at a children's theatre." She fluffs the wig a little, even though it's pretty fluffy already. "It's hard out there for an outfit that wants to stay in business. But you have something that a bar like the Pick n' Play doesn't, and that's called goodwill. People like a children's theatre. You just have to make them want to pay for it like they want to pay for a whiskey sour, you heck of a grandson, you. Now where's your dad? We'll be late if he doesn't put down that paintbrush and get down the road."

"Nothing wrong with a little hard work, Vee," Dad calls from wherever he is. "Isn't that right, Sid?"

Gram goes off to find Dad. You can hear a set of keys jingling and then the truck starts up. They drive off, and I can just about hear some singing as they go down the street. Dad might drive to the Pick n' Play, but you couldn't get him on that stage for anything. I once told Folly I'd pay cash money to see my dad sing karaoke, but Folly said that was a losing investment.

Act II

SCENE TWO

(Scene Two starts off in Folly's toolshed, and I'm hoping I won't fall down in this scene.)

I look over to Folly's garden and see him opening the door to his office. It might look like a toolshed from the outside, and there might be a couple of rusty shovels and rakes and things leaning against the wall in there, but it's the headquarters of Folly's whole operation. He waves me over.

"It's here," he says, and his eyes are shining the way they did when he got a signed letter from the head teacher congratulating him on his perfect attendance since kindergarten.

"What's here?"

"Our delivery. Our useful household products. Our goods, wares, stock-in-trade, merchandise, commodities. Our articles, saleables, vendibles." He's got that lovesick look again. "Our *stuff*." Our teacher last year said if there was one shred of poetry in Folly's soul, it entered through his wallet.

Inside the shed, there's a stack of eight cardboard boxes. Each of them has a sticker on it that says *Marked for Destruction*.

"What does that mean?" I ask, because it might be something that business people like Folly and Zap Zapter know and suckers like me don't.

"You know what that means? It means we're going to destroy the competition, that's what. No one's going to touch us at selling useful household products on Hatahatchee Street."

I don't tell him no one else is going to try selling useful household products on Hatahatchee Street because they're all too embarrassed to join the Little Trixie Commerce Club. Even the Girl Scouts will probably laugh at us while they go along selling their cookies.

"I didn't tell my mum about this," Folly says. "I want it to be a surprise when I show her how much money I made, and I'll give some to her so she can make a better investment this time."

"Isn't your mum going to be scared of investments?" I ask.

"Don't be scared, be prepared," says Folly, and he takes a pair of scissors from his desk, which, if you didn't know better, would look a lot like a couple of wooden crates and a door. He says a lot of young entrepreneurs make their desks out of doors.

"What kind of stuff do you think they sent?" I ask as Folly slices through the packing tape. "I hope it's not just cleaning products."

Folly whistles. "You can make great profits on that stuff. It's mostly water. You just add a few cents' worth of chemicals."

He pulls the flaps open and takes out a notebook. The whole box is full of notebooks. They're all just the same, about the size of our school notebooks, with black plastic covers.

"Maybe these are instructions or something?"

Folly flips one of the books open. It's empty. The pages are lined with rows and columns. It looks familiar, but I don't place it until Folly makes a soft gurgle in his throat and says, "It's a ledger. You use it to record your business purchases and your income."

Of course I recognize it now. That book looks just the way Folly talks.

I slice open a couple of other boxes: more ledgers. I don't bother taking them out of the boxes.

"They want us to sell ledgers to people?" I ask. "Eight boxes of them? Most people don't have businesses."

"Oh, you can use these for your home bookkeeping, too," says Folly, like I know anything about home bookkeeping. "Everyone needs a way to record their finances."

I want to trust Folly, because it's what I've done ever since I met him. He's the sort of person you just believe in. But I had my doubts about this business enterprise from the start, and now that I see what Little Trixie wants us to sell, I'm a double doubter. "You'd better ask for your money back, Folly. We can't sell this stuff. We'll look like we robbed the Office Star store."

Have you ever seen a play where the light suddenly changes, and you know that something good is about to happen? Maybe one actor gets a spotlight on them, and you can almost hear the speech coming? Well, no kidding, the light does change just then. The clouds finally pull apart the way they do after a thunderstorm, and a spotlight comes straight from the heart of the sun all the way down 93 million miles and through the window in the toolshed to light up Folly King's face. Cue the angel choir sound effect.

"Of course we can sell them," he says. He pulls at his bow tie, which looks almost golden in the sun. "We're salesmen."

I'd leave the scene right there because it's so perfect, and because Folly is standing still and staring into the distance like he expects the curtain to close in front of him, but I have to be real for a second. "It's going to be tough," I say.

Folly just leans on his busted-up old door-desk and smiles at me. "Sure it's going to be tough. But you have to learn the rules. First thing is, you have to know your market."

"Don't you have to know the thing you're trying to sell first?" I ask. "Then you work out who you're trying to sell it to?"

"The thing you've got to understand about business is, it's all about people. Doesn't matter if you're selling bleach or basketballs. So we have to look around us, see who's out there."

"May's out there," I say, because through the doorway I can see her standing in my back garden wearing a pair of yellow rubber gloves. I'd say she's wearing them to help her get into character for something, but any role that comes with rubber gloves is not a role May wants to have.

I turn back to Folly, who's got a goofy smile on his face. He goes to look out the door. "May?" But she and her rubber gloves are gone. Folly clears his throat, and he's all business again. "Not May, Sid. She doesn't have any money. That's the part about your *market*. Those are the people who have some cash to spare. Everyone else is just people."

I am starting to see that some of this sales talk is kind

of like the theatre. You're trying to convince someone of something that maybe they would never have thought about until you came along and said so. And Folly's been in sales since the day he was born.

"Are we going to sell them to all your egg customers?"

"We're going to have to branch out. The egg business is okay for starters, but it's not reliable like consumer goods are. I swear those chickens aren't laying like they used to. I went in there yesterday and got maybe half the eggs I was expecting."

"Maybe they're sick."

Just like they were waiting for their cue, the chickens start squawking and bawking. When they all get going, you can hear them all across the neighbourhood.

"I don't know. But what I'm thinking with this new product line is, we want to target people who fit certain demographics.

"What kind of people want to buy ledger books?" He flips a page on the giant pad of paper he's got on an easel in the corner. "I'll make a pie chart."

He draws a big circle, divides it into pie slices, and colours them in blue and red and green. On the blue part of the pie, he writes OFFICE WORKERS. "Office workers always need ledgers," says Folly. "It's a significant business need. So that's part of our market."

He marks the red slice of pie HOME BUSINESS

OWNERS. "Lots of people work from home," says Folly. "Like Mr J. I bet he'll buy some of these."

And on the green part, Folly writes, OTHER. That's the smallest part of the pie. "What's 'other'?"

"'Other' is everyone else. That's for when we make contacts out of people who don't fall into our two main groups. People who just like keeping accurate records of their money. And who doesn't like that?"

"Why wouldn't people just use computers or something?" Now that I think about it, I've seen Ruben sit down with a laptop after he counts out the box office cash drawer.

Folly considers that for a second. He doesn't say anything, but I know he'll have an answer ready when a customer asks him the same question.

I can't work out why Little Trixie would want kids to go around selling ledgers to people. That's worse than calendars, worse than magazine subscriptions or oven gloves or any other thing you could sell. Folly's some kind of optimist, thinking we can just find some OFFICE WORKERS and OTHER people and start raking in the cash. I ought to write Little Trixie a letter of complaint. We learned how to do that in citizenship class last year.

He tacks his chart up on the wall and says, "Let's do a practice run. You be you, going down the street selling ledgers, and I'll be a customer. Got it?"

"Sure."

"Hang on. You need something." He looks me over, then unclips his bow tie and clips it to my collar. "Now you're ready. Go."

I knock on the side of the shed. "Do you want to buy some ledgers?"

Folly shakes his head. "We need to work on your technique, Sid. You're not one of those charity car washes. You're a reputable businessman. You're one-half of King and Camazzola, and you're acting like a numbskull. Now." He pulls at the sleeves of my T-shirt and tries to flatten the front part of my hair.

"Hey, I like my hair the way it is!"

"But your customers don't. Pull your shorts up, and give me your best smile."

I shoot him a grin, one that I think shows every last one of my teeth, which are looking pretty white these days on account of brushing them with bicarbonate of soda.

"Oh no, man. That's got to change. Watch this." Folly takes a breath, and then his face relaxes into an easy, open smile. He only shows about five teeth, which I think is missing an opportunity. "I call this one the Classic. Go on, you try."

I slide my lips back and tilt my head just a little like Folly did, and I hold it like I'm posing for a picture.

"Maybe you're not ready for the Classic. That is more of a level-two look. Try this one." He opens his eyes a tiny bit wider than usual and smiles with his lips closed. "That's the Boy Scout. You wear that face, you're ready for anything."

I clamp my lips shut and curl them up, and I go for a kind of startled rabbit look around the eyes. Folly puts a hand over his face.

"You know what I'm thinking about when I do the Boy Scout?"

I shake my head. My eyes are getting tired from not blinking.

"I'm thinking that I have been put here on this earth to save people. Maybe I'm only saving them from the heartache of missing out on one of the greatest office supply deals this side of Pensacola, but it's the saving part that shows up on your face. You have to feel like you're doing someone some good in the world."

I try to feel like that, like I'm doing some good. And then I remember – I do people good all the time. What did Mr Jameson say? *Above average.* My face relaxes when I think of Mr. Jameson and I blink, and Folly breaks out with some other smile I don't know the name of. "That's it, Sid! You got it! You look like that, no one's going to say no to you."

"Excuse me, sir, I'm selling these ledgers–" I start to say.

Folly cuts in. "Business solutions. No – *financial accountability* solutions. That's what we're going to call them."

"But they're ledgers."

"I know that. But you have to understand, people want

97

someone to solve their problems for them. So that's what we're selling. Solutions."

"I'm selling financial accountability solutions. Do you want to buy some?"

"Spoo," says Folly.

I'll admit it. I am taken aback. "Spoon?" I say, in case maybe he's got it wrong.

Folly clears his throat. "SPOO, I said. Smile, Personalize, Observe, Objectify."

"Is that like the SQUAT thing you were talking about when you started selling eggs?" Folly must have a hundred and fifty of Zap Zapter's business acronyms lodged up there in his brain.

"That was SWOT. Strengths, Weaknesses, Opportunities, Threats. That's when you work out how to crush your competition. This is different. You got the smile part, now you have to personalize. You know how you do that?"

"How?"

"You call me by my name."

I can do that. "Hey, Folly, do you want to buy some of these business solutions?"

"Not like that. You do it like a man with some pride in himself. Pretend I'm someone else. What's Mr Jameson's name?"

"Mr Jameson."

"His first name! You clean a man's chicken coop, and

you don't even know his first name? Fine, just call him Mr Jameson."

"This SPOO thing is tough, Folly. Let me try again." I get my above-average smile on and knock on the air this time, because my knuckles are getting splinters from this old toolshed. "Excuse me, Mr Jameson, how would you like to buy some of these *financial accountability* solutions I'm selling here?"

Folly takes on a deep voice and puffs himself up a little. "Kid, I have all the financial accountability solutions I need."

"Oh, okay. Maybe some other time."

Folly slaps his forehead. "Not *Oh, okay, maybe some other time*. No! You have three tries to make the sale, Sid. First try, you do your thing, and if that doesn't work, you have to change your game. You identify a need, and you go for that." He starts talking in a smooth voice that sounds about three sizes too big for him. I'm going to call it the Zap Junior voice. "It's just that I know the importance of keeping accurate and up-to-date records, sir, and you never know when the tax man is going to come knocking on your door."

"Am I the tax man now?" I get ready to knock again.

We have so many characters in this toolshed, I'm going to have to write it out like a script.

                    FOLLY

        No. Just pay attention. If your second
           try doesn't work, you go for the
                  scarcity angle.

                   ZAP JUNIOR

          I only have a few of these at this
        price, sir. It would be a real shame to
               pass up a good deal.

                     FOLLY

        That's how you close a deal. You have
        to have a close, you see? That's how you
        get the customer on your hook and close
        the sale. There are lots of different
        closes, but we're going to save that
               lesson for another day.

                      ME

                    I see.

Except I don't see. I don't see why we're trying to start this crazy business, and I don't see what we're going to get out of it except a lot of ledgers sitting around in the toolshed forever. The End.

With Folly, it's never The End. There's always something else to try. "No you don't. That's why you need some real live practice. Come on."

"But we didn't even get to OO, Folly. We didn't get past the spuh part."

I start unclipping Folly's bow tie from my shirt, but he says, "Leave it. You're going to need it."

Act II

SCENE THREE

(*Over at Mr Jameson's again, but this time we get to go inside.*)

Mr Jameson's sitting on his front porch, swirling the last of his iced tea around in his tall glass. "Well, hello, gentlemen," he says when we turn up his path. Folly's put a couple of extra ledgers in his briefcase and I'm carrying the display model, the one we were looking at back in the office. He says you can't show all your stock, or people will think you're desperate to get rid of it and try to talk your price down. So we're taking orders for expedited delivery. Expedited, I think, means "as soon as we get back to the toolshed".

Folly sticks his hand out to Mr Jameson and turns on the

Classic. "What a beautiful day we're having, sir. Nothing better than enjoying it with a glass of iced tea, am I right?"

Mr Jameson's got a Classic of his own, and when he shakes Folly's hand I almost want to take a picture of them for the cover of a magazine. "You are right, Mr King. What can I do for you?"

Folly slips into the Boy Scout. "Oh, no, sir. I was hoping to do something for you. You see, Sid and I have recently branched out from the egg business into the office supply sector, and of all the residents on this fine street, we wanted you to be the first to benefit from this turn of events."

"I'm honoured," says Mr Jameson. "What particular part of the office supply sector have you decided to apply your skills to?"

This is where I come in. I remember what Folly said: lead into it gracefully. Don't ask directly if your customer wants to buy. Of course they want to buy, he told me. People are itching to buy stuff. It's just got to be the right stuff. Our job is to make what we have the right stuff.

"You seem like a very, uh, accurate type of person," I say. "And what's more important these days to people who value accuracy than–" I struggle to remember the words Folly told me to use. "Than financial accountability. What's more important than financial accountability? You, uh, have a lot of finances you need to account for?"

I'm supposed to be reeling Mr Jameson in, but it doesn't feel like he's even on the end of my line. His eyes don't light up with interest, that's for sure. He looks down at the display model. "Is that your financial accountability product, Sid?"

"Solution," I say. "It's called a financial accountability solution." I can feel the heat from Folly's smile. "This is it."

"Let me take a look at it." I hand the ledger to Mr Jameson, and Folly sucks in a quick breath, which I am pretty sure is not a sound he wants to be heard making. "Is this the only solution you have, or are there more?"

"We have eight boxes of them," I say before I remember about scarcity.

"And how did you happen to get your hands on eight boxes of bookkeeping ledgers?"

This time Folly answers. "We're card-carrying members of the Little Trixie Commerce Club, sir. We made an investment in useful household goods, and this is it. Would you like to see our card?" He goes to his shorts pocket to pull out the card.

"No, no, that's all right. I believe you. When I was a kid, we sold chocolate bars. Don't they have any chocolate bars to sell in this Little Trixie Club?"

"This is the twenty-first century," Folly says. "We're selling what the modern consumer wants. Paper's making a comeback. Folks are getting tired of staring at screens all day. You don't want to be left out in the cold without a paper ledger, do you?"

I don't know if Folly's telling the truth, or just saying what he wants to be the truth. But it sounds good.

"I would hate to be behind the times," says Mr Jameson.

"Why don't you come in and we'll continue this discussion over some iced tea, like civilized people."

"Sure." We follow Mr Jameson into his house. It has the same kind of smell that all the houses on Hatahatchee Street have, like a cave would smell if it was done up in linoleum. But it's also got a better smell on top of that – coffee and cinnamon.

The thing I like most about his house is that almost everything is at just his level. He's got high shelves, but there's nothing on the top of them. Even all his pictures are down where he can look at them best, and everyone else has to bend over a little and make themselves fit.

There's one picture on his wall that I bend over to get a good look at. It's the one of him in his dress uniform standing next to Mrs Jameson. Mr Jameson's coat fits him like it was made for him, and maybe it was. It's dark blue with a row of gold buttons and a silver bar on the shoulder. Mrs Jameson's about as pretty as a grown-up woman could be, with her hair in a coil of braids on top of her head and a silver dress that I know May would die for. Mrs Jameson's got her hand on Mr Jameson's arm, and they look like instead of staring at the camera, they really want to be staring at each other. Mr Jameson catches me, and he backs up. "I suppose a card-carrying business type like you is too busy to help me look for that other picture now, huh, Sid?"

"Oh, no, I'll still help. I have lots of time."

Mr Jameson's got his laptop set up at the kitchen table,

next to a box of cookies. The screen shows a picture of a pig, a cookie and good old Miss Alabama Harper, this time with a purple streak in her hair. "I'm doing her website," he says, "but I'm a little stuck on how to advertise this new cookie she's come up with. Who would think you could buy cookies on the internet? But I suppose people do."

"Oh, you can buy anything on the internet," Folly practically sings, never mind what he was just saying about paper and screens. "I'm already thinking of how we can expand our business to include an online component. Door-to-door is just for starters. You have to pound the ground before you can fly the sky. Zap Zapter was a door-to-door man for four years before he even got a phone line."

"Sound advice," says Mr Jameson. "I can't tell you how many people have asked me to build their website, and they hardly even know what their business is about."

"Now, you have to have a business plan," Folly says, but before he can start another lecture, I give him my version of the Classic, just to shock his mind out of its track.

"So tell me more about financial accountability, gentlemen," says Mr Jameson.

I'm still clutching the display model, which Folly pries out of my hands. "When your customers pay you, you write it down in here. No batteries required. I'll even throw in a free pen." He opens his briefcase and takes out the extra ledgers he brought, just in case Mr Jameson wanted to get the bulk discount, and hunts around for a pen.

I pick up one of the spare ledgers and flip through it. The pages are full of someone's handwriting. They sent us a used ledger.

"Hey, Folly," I say, showing it to him. "This one's been written in." I really ought to write Little Trixie a letter of complaint. He takes it, and I open another one. It's been used too.

Folly looks at the page and looks confused for a second, but then his eyes go wide and his legs start to shake. He reads, "'Paper clips. Property insurance. Doughnuts for staff meeting day.' It's Little Trixie's bookkeeping." The way he says it, he means *It's the Dead Sea Scrolls I've discovered right here in Mr J.'s kitchen.*

"Huh," says Mr Jameson again. "Where did you say you got this from?"

"The Little Trixie Commerce Club," I say. "We thought they were all blank."

"I think you'd better send this back to Little Trixie, Folly. This looks like their bookkeeping records. I think they've sent this by mistake. You say you have eight boxes of these?"

I nod.

"I don't know how they got so mixed up, but I'll bet they'll be happy to have this back. Do you want to use my phone to give them a call?"

"I suppose we'd better," I say, but Folly starts going way off script. He's talking like his lines were handed down to him by Zap Zapter himself.

"No, sir, we can take care of this ourselves. I am very

sorry to say that we won't be able to fulfil your order at this time, but we will connect with you again once our product lines have been secured going forward. As Vice President of Accounting and Procurement at King and Camazzola, I am going to remedy this disfortunate situation as soon as time permits, and thank you very much for your time today, sir." He takes the ledger and turns for the door.

I tell you what, when Folly uses a made-up word like *disfortunate*, it means he's got something on his mind.

"Do you want me to come with you?" I say, because that's what a good business partner would do. But Folly shakes his head, unclips the tie from my shirt and puts it back on his own, and says, "Why don't you and Mr J. talk about our website while I go and, uh, pack all this stuff up so we can, uh." He doesn't finish what he's saying to me, but to Mr Jameson, he says, "I'm going to leave you with our Vice President of Online Services. He's going to discuss the future with you."

I know Folly means websites and e-this-and-that, but when he says the word *future* I get a picture of the actual future, just a couple of months down the line, where all the Juicebox kids are rehearsing for the autumn play, and maybe Ruben's showing me how to work the bank of lights from the control panel at the back of the house. It's like the present is at stage left, and the future's being set up over at stage right, and it's just a few steps to get there but it takes forever. "Do you want to discuss the future, Sid?" Mr Jameson asks when Folly's gone.

My future-vision swings back to now. "Sure," I say. "Ten minutes from now is the future, right? Let's talk about how I'm going to look for that picture and how maybe you'll give me one of those cookies as a thank you."

Mr Jameson laughs. "That's a good kind of future to have in mind."

I start hunting up in the high places, on the tops of his shelves, in his high cabinets, but there's nothing up there. I look under stuff and at the back of places where it might be hard for him to get in and look, and there's still nothing. After a while he wheels up to me and says, "Hey, there, Sid. Why don't you crawl out of that corner and come and have a seat on the front porch?"

He's already got the jug of iced tea on a tray on his lap and the box of cookies next to it. He doesn't have to tell me twice.

"Alabama sent me this box so I could taste one of every kind of cookie she makes and capture its true essence on her website. That's what she said, anyway." He picks one up and breaks it in half. "Try this. What do you think its true essence is?"

I can see from the marks on the box that its true essence is kind of greasy. I take a bite. Good thing this is the theatre and you can't taste what I'm tasting right now.

"What kind is this?" I ask, struggling to swallow because I don't want to spit out my food like a baby in front of Mr Jameson.

"She calls it the Hog Farmer."

That is one unappetizing name for an unappetizing cookie. Mr Jameson picks up a sheet of paper and reads from it. "'The Hog Farmer is a chocolate cookie with a teensy little bit of bacon dripping in there.' That's her description, but I'm supposed to come up with something more suited to the internet age."

"Like what?"

"Like I don't have a clue. Maybe I'll ask your business partner the next time I see him. Anyway." He swats a fly away, breathes a great big thoughtful sigh, and links his hands together behind his head. "Do you know what the funny thing is? I don't think you're going to find that picture in my house."

"But I'm looking everywhere I can think of. I even looked under all your towels and stuff."

"Exactly. Why's my very favourite picture of all time going to be underneath my towels? Or way at the back of the cabinet under the bathroom sink?"

"But where else is it going to be?"

"That's the mystery, Sid. I don't know where. I had it in a frame next to my bed, and then I brought it out to show a few people, and I kept it there in the living room for a little while because—" I can hear the tears that are trying to come out behind his words. "Because we used to like to watch TV together. She loved those forensic dramas, you know? So sometimes I sit with her picture, and – I used to sit with her picture. But I know I didn't move it out of the living room. I *know* I didn't."

He stares into his glass. A half-slice of lemon is floating on the surface of the tea, like a little rowing boat with nowhere to go.

"I don't want to stop looking for it," I say. "I want to help you find it."

"I won't stop you from looking," he says. "But I might stop myself from hoping."

That is the saddest thing I've heard all day, and I've heard Folly King coaching his numbskull friend on how to smile.

"Can I ask you a question?" I say. "I know I didn't clean the coop today, but–"

"You can ask any question you want, Sid. You have unlimited question privileges with me."

"It's just I don't want you to give up hope." That might not look like a question, but I mean it that way. Because I know how much effort it takes to hope that hard, and sometimes it's a big question if you can keep up the effort. But if he can keep it up, then maybe I can, too.

"No? Don't worry, I don't really mean it. But you know how it feels when you think you might have lost something forever. Or maybe you don't. Maybe you're too young to know what that feels like."

"No, sir," I say. "I know just what it feels like. I know I don't want to lose the Juicebox forever." Because all my future-vision might just be future-wishing if we can't get enough money, and this whole Little Trixie mix-up isn't helping.

Then I worry that I'm making a theatre sound as important as a person, and Mr Jameson might not appreciate that. Even though to me, the Juicebox is like a living thing. "I don't mean–" I start to say, but Mr Jameson gives me a pat on the shoulder.

"It's okay. You feel how you feel. You don't ever have to apologize for that."

We finish our glasses of tea and split a couple more cookies, one with jam in the middle, which makes me think of Jelly Baby, and one with raisins that Miss Alabama Harper calls a Squashed Bug cookie, which makes me think of Beatrice the Cockroach. And then I see what I didn't see before, because it was hidden under a bunch of other cookies: a meringue with a tiny chocolate chip on the top. It doesn't stand as straight as May and it's probably buckets sweeter than she is, but it's got her name written all over it.

A whole new world of questions opens up: Is this why May's always riding into town with her meringues? So that Miss Alabama Harper can sell them at Panhandle Pastries? But why? And why won't May tell anyone about it, and what kind of money is she making, and is she going to give any of it to the Juicebox, or use it to buy ledgers so we can make a big charitable donation to the theatre? And why would May need a bunch of ledgers anyway?

I am only saved from a minor brain explosion due to all this speculating when Mr Jameson refills my glass and says, "Now, the meringue is a tiny miracle of engineering. The whole reason jet engines don't melt is because they build them like meringues."

And by the time he's finished talking about air pockets and melting points and things, I've almost forgotten about May.

Almost. But when I get home, May's hard at work in the kitchen, whipping up those egg whites like she sees my face in the bottom of the bowl. There's a long red scratch on her arm. I have at least a drop of sense in my squirrel head, though, so I don't ask her what she's doing selling meringues to Miss Alabama Harper. She's already got a look on her face that says, "Why don't you go and kiss a chicken, Sid?" And there's probably worse up the sleeve of her tank top for later.

Act II

SCENE FOUR

(It's a few days later, and we're back at the Juicebox. But you would have realized that pretty fast.)

The Juicebox does two plays in the autumn and two in the spring, and most years we do one in the summer, too. But this year, because of having no money, Ruben's just doing theatre camp and special fundraisers like the variety show. Theatre camp is where we do practice exercises and don't use any sets and don't sell any concessions. Even Pen's here, because it's all ages and she doesn't have to memorize any lines. Folly wouldn't give theatre camp the time of day except that he can see the serious trouble we're in, and he's offered to do more than just run our concession stand. He's having his own personal Fundraising Camp. It's win-win, according to Folly. He gets another opportunity to do some LTN, and we get the benefit of his business acumen.

I said the word *acumen* sounds like a kind of car, which really would help us out, but Folly said it just means he's smart.

Folly and I are sitting on the edge of the stage with Ruben, watching the actors do exercises. They're all on the carpet where the audience would be sitting, if we had an audience. The folding chairs are leaning against the walls, and the house lights are up. Even in the middle of the day, we have to use the lights, because the windows are covered with plywood and heavy curtains.

"The variety show was supposed to save our butts, but it did not save our butts," says Ruben. He's got on a T-shirt with paint splatters all over it, like he's already mentally painting boat bottoms.

The kids finish an improv exercise, where they just make stuff up on the fly, and then they start mirroring, where they pretend that one of them is the mirror reflection of the other one. Noah raises his right hand, and Brandon raises his left at almost the same time, but you can tell who moved first. When you get really good, no one can tell. It's like a living mirror.

"We need to plan for our next season," says Ruben.

"You need to earn more revenue," says Folly.

"I'll have to make the sets."

"You have to make some money."

"In the theatre–"

"In business–"

Because I don't want this going on all day, I step all over their lines and say, "I bet Folly has some great ideas. Right, Folly?"

For a businessman, Folly's pretty good at improv. "You should have an Amateur Night," he says. "Because the variety show was good, but that's all stuff people have seen before. You want to offer something new, and you've got to give your customer base a two-point-oh experience."

"What's that?" I say, because I guess Ruben doesn't know either, and I don't mind looking like the dumb one.

"It's when you let your customers participate, so they're not just sitting and watching a load of long speeches and giant insects." If anyone else said that, I'd be furious, but Folly is the master of how to tell it like it is without getting anyone's feathers ruffled. Like I said, he barely even ruffles the chickens' feathers.

"There is something to be said for sitting and watching," says Ruben slowly, "and those soliloquies, they have their place, but I see what you mean. We sell tickets, and the audience gives us a show. You have your head screwed on tightly, Folly."

Folly nods, like it's just common knowledge about his head. "Hardly costs you a thing."

"That's even better than my karaoke idea," I say.

Ruben groans, but not in a mean way. "Karaoke would bring your grandmother to the Juicebox," he says. "But it will take more than an old lady in a wig to save this theatre."

And then he must see that I'm about to launch into my own soliloquy about the importance of wigs and grandmothers, because he adds, "I love your grandmother. You know that. Of all the singing old ladies in wigs, she is by far my favourite."

Mine too.

"So, all right, Folly. Make an advertisement for Amateur Night, and we'll send it to the *Hatahatchee Times-Star*. Two dollars a ticket?"

"Five," says Folly.

Ruben nods and goes to give the kids another exercise.

"See, you're already good at finances," I tell Folly. "You didn't need those Little Trixie ledgers."

Folly clears his throat. I'm so used to him looking as clean as if he's just stepped out of a car wash, it takes a minute for me to realize what that look on his face is saying: guilt.

"You didn't send them back, did you?"

"I started looking through more of those ledgers, Sid. I was curious. There were a couple of blank ones, but all the others were filled out. There's everything about the Little Trixie company in those books. And there's other stuff, too. Some of the boxes had binders and notebooks. I'm going through everything, learning about the whole business."

"If we don't send them back, how are they going to know to send us the right stuff? No one's going to buy a lot of used ledgers and notebooks." Probably no one wants unused ledgers, either, at least not enough of them to help out the Juicebox.

If I know Folly, he'll do whatever it takes to get his money back. He might be a kind of fool, but it's not the broke kind.

"What? No, I paid good money for them. I'm going to learn everything I can, and then maybe I'll send them back. I have to know this stuff if I'm going to have my own business."

"Learn? Like what?"

Folly opens his briefcase, and for once he's got something in there besides the business cards he wrote out himself. He's got his mum's laptop and a stack of Little Trixie's ledgers. He takes one out and opens it up. When he gets to the right page, he says, "Like here. This is a record from July 2012. Here's assets – that's what they own – and here's liabilities – that's what they owe. That number there – $351,469. See how it's in the assets column?"

Folly jabs at the writing like he wants to get it off the page and floating around the room like he's in some high-tech crime show.

"Look, that's how much money they make from subscriptions. And here's what they spend on paper. And ink. And here's what they pay their staff. I'm learning everything there is to know about Little Trixie, from the inside. See, down here all the numbers add up, and that's called equity. It's their profit." Folly gets out another book.

"But there's other stuff, too, about how many kids are in the club, what the members pay Little Trixie for the stuff they sell, and then how much they sell it to the consumer for."

There's a whole list of kids' names and addresses and the date they joined the Commerce Club. It even says how much they sold.

"I don't think we should be looking at this," I say. "You remember how we learned to be good digital citizens in Ms Kwan's class."

"This isn't digital. That's the whole point."

I try again. "And you're always going on about business ethics."

That's done it. This is the kind of major moral crisis that looks so good onstage. I'm thinking I'd use a back light and gently rising music. Folly plays it up, too. There's a little bit of Frankie's sense of drama in him after all. He turns his head, squares his shoulders and exhales. "You just might be right," he says. "Zap Zapter says you have to keep your head above the water if you don't want the algae in your ears. Or if you want to earn the Golden Bow Tie award."

Well, I suppose that must be true.

Folly closes the ledger. "Maybe I will send these back. I can learn about bookkeeping with one of those online tutorials. And you know what?" he says, looking up at me. "I bet Little Trixie's going to be pretty happy with me when I tell them about this. Maybe," and he lies back on the stage like he's watching for fireworks, "maybe they'll even give me a reward. Maybe I'll be Little Trixie Salesman of the Month. No. No, wait." He folds his hands behind his head and closes his eyes. "Salesman of the Year."

I could leave Folly like that for a week and a half and come back and find him just the same way, so I go on over and say hi to Jelly Baby, since everyone's taking a break from the warm-up games.

"Why do you go by Jelly Baby?" I ask, because a director ought to be direct. "Is that some kind of Cuban sweet?"

"It's an English sweet." She digs around in her pocket and brings out a little bag of sweets and holds it out to me. I choose a red one. It's a little sugar-dusted person, and it tastes like some kind of berry. "My mum's English. She sends them to me every year for my birthday."

"I thought you were an . . ." But I can't say it.

Jelly Baby snorts. "An orphan? No, Beatrice just made that up. My mum lived in Florida for a while, but when my parents split up, she went back to England and stayed over there."

"Oh." I don't know how to talk about what it's like to have a mum so far away, but I can keep talking about sweets. "So you like those sweets so much you named yourself after them?"

"Kind of. When I was little, I thought they looked like little puppets, and I loved puppets, and there you go."

I want to ask her how someone decides they love puppets, because it seems like a weird thing to love, but maybe you don't decide what you love. I love the theatre, and someone might think that's weird, too.

Ruben walks over to us. "Doña Juliana Rosa," he says, "I forgot to bring down the snacks from upstairs. Will you and Sir Sidney with the Silly Hair please bring them?" He ruffles my hair so it gets even more in my eyes.

"Ooh, snacks," says Jelly Baby, and she heads up to Ruben's apartment, which must be the greatest apartment on earth if it's right above the greatest theatre in Hatahatchee.

Going up the stairs, I feel like I'm in one of those celebrity shows, where you see inside a famous singer's house and they show you their built-in aquarium full of exotic fish and a hundred containers of non-fat yogurt in their fridge. I know Ruben's apartment isn't going to be like that, but I hope whatever it looks like, it's going to tell me something about how my life will be when I'm grown up like he is. The thing I can't work out is how I'm ever going to be the director of the Juicebox, since I also hope that Ruben never ever moves away.

Jelly Baby opens the door, and we go in. The first thing I see is that Ruben has a small fish tank with one ordinary-looking fish in it, and that makes me feel just fine. I couldn't live up to a built-in aquarium lifestyle, anyway.

Then I notice the posters from different plays and musicals on the walls. I recognize some of the names – *Hamilton* and *The Lion King* – but I've never seen any of them. That's okay. I will one day. Folly's already promised to drive me to New York and drop me off on Broadway on his way to Wall Street.

There's a giant wooden crate in Ruben's living room that looks like it could hold a dead body if it had to. It's got *S.W.I.Z.* stencilled on each side in big letters, and underneath that in tiny letters it says *South-Western Industrial Zips*.

Jelly Baby goes to the kitchen and comes out with a bowl of crisps and some guacamole. She catches me looking at the crate.

"That's a lot of zips," I say. I bet Folly could sell all those zips in a heartbeat. "Are you a travelling salesman, too?"

"I'm a travelling sales*person*," she says.

"Really?"

She grins. "No. But Doña Flor always travels in a box marked with something like that on it."

"Like a disguise?" I say. Which is funny if you think about it: Doña Flor is like a disguise that has its own disguise.

"Yeah. My great-grandfather used to do that, and he made me promise I would, too."

"Did he give you Doña Flor?"

I want to ask her to open the box so I can look at how the puppet works, but I get the feeling that getting up close and personal with the big puppet is kind of like

Folly showing you the one picture he owns of his Pap-Pap standing next to that BMW. A rare and valuable thing.

The way Jelly Baby moved Doña Flor around, it was like they were the same person, and I don't know for sure but I think it must take some real skill to do that. I've seen talent onstage, like when May lets fly with a song or Ruben gets one of the actors to *inhabit* their character, like he's always saying they should do. But what Jelly Baby did at the variety show goes past talent. It's like when I'm riding my bike over to Turkey Bayou to jump off the tyre swing and I catch sight of a pelican just dipping into the water. It doesn't look easy, being a pelican with that big sack of a beak, but you watch it for a minute, and you know it looks *right*.

Jelly Baby puts the food down. "He *made* Doña Flor, and before he died, he gave her to me. He was a famous puppeteer. He used to do shows all around Cuba, telling stories and jokes, or making fun of the government."

"I thought puppets were just to entertain little kids." But I think of Doña Flor and how different she is from any puppet I've ever seen.

"Puppets do all kinds of things," says Jelly Baby. "They can do and say things that people would get into trouble for. My great-grandfather said a puppet can tease a king, but a man will lose his head.

"But someone didn't like what my great-grandfather was saying, even though he was using Doña Flor to say it. They knew he couldn't say the same things if he wasn't speaking through her, so they tried to smash her up. He started disguising her crate whenever he had to travel, and then he gave her to me, and now I do the same thing."

I can tell how much Doña Flor means to Jelly Baby. It's not just something she uses to perform. It's more than that. "It's like she's *real*, but she's not alive," I say.

"I think it's the other way around," says Jelly Baby. "She's alive, but she's not real."

I think about that while Jelly Baby swings open the front of the wooden crate. I'm going to be thinking about that for a while.

Inside the crate is a huge leather suitcase. Jelly Baby unzips it, and I see Doña Flor's head and a couple of sticks coming out from the yards and yards of yellow fabric. Doña Flor's wearing a new dress, made from the yellow curtain Jelly Baby put on me at the variety show. I'm big enough to say it looks better on Doña Flor.

"These are her bones," says Jelly Baby. "There's a helmet thing that I wear, and that controls her head. Then I hold the sticks to move her arms. It's all really delicate."

"How do you see out of that head?"

"There are tiny holes, so I can see something if it's right in front of me, but I can't see anything to the sides."

"And how does it talk?" I mean, I realize it's only Jelly Baby talking. That came out wrong.

She laughs. "There's a mechanism that carries your voice, otherwise I'd have to shout and you still wouldn't be able to understand me."

Jelly Baby closes the case.

"She's amazing. She's like something in a museum," I say.

She smiles. "Yeah, I know. My great-grandfather could make anything. He made me some hand puppets and rod puppets, and then finally he gave me Doña Flor. She was his favourite."

There's another, smaller puppet, a clown in an orange costume, hanging on strings from a hook on the wall. All the strings are tied to two long sticks. Jelly Baby picks up the sticks and lets the clown rest its feet on the floor. "This is another one he made. He gave her to Ruben." She lifts her arms and the clown jumps. She sways her arms, and the clown dances from side to side. "Marionettes are hard to operate. Anyone can make them do this kind of stuff, but it takes a lot of practice to get them to move like they're–"

"Like they're not real, but they're alive?"

Jelly Baby smiles. "Yeah."

"Why'd you bring Doña Flor here, if she's so valuable? I mean, what if something happened to her?"

That happy look goes away and Jelly Baby says, "My dad was trying to send me to stay with a lot of different relatives this summer, but I only wanted to come here, because Ruben said I could spend the whole summer in the theatre. I told my dad, 'Wherever I go, Doña Flor goes, too.' And it's expensive to ship Doña Flor. He doesn't understand me, or puppets, but he understands money."

It seems like money's at the bottom of every problem we have this summer.

"I'm glad you came here. You were pretty great at the variety show," I tell her, but as soon as I say it, I know "great" isn't the right word.

"Thanks," says Jelly Baby. "Too bad we didn't make much."

"We will," I say. "I just know it." I'm saying it even if I'm not feeling it, because Folly has another saying, but I bet Ruben would like it, too: Fake it till you make it.

"You really love this place, don't you?" says Jelly Baby.

Maybe it doesn't look like much compared to a fancy Miami grown-up theatre, but it's what I've got. "I do," I say. And then I say, "You should stay here forever."

Folly would probably say I should try a more subtle sales pitch, but I don't care. I like Jelly Baby, and I think she likes the theatre as much as I do. We need more people around here who care about things like she does.

"I wish I could. I'm probably going to move to England with my mum at the end of the summer. Or I'll stay in Miami with my dad. They're kind of fighting about it."

"Do you want to go to England? That's so far away."

Jelly Baby shrugs, and even though she's not really an orphan, or even pretending to be one like I was, I think maybe she knows better than I do how to inhabit that character.

We go back downstairs and put out the snacks for

everyone. Then it's back to exercises. The next exercise we do is called Props. Ruben gives everyone a partner and a prop, and they have to come up with some kind of scene about the prop. The worst props always make the best scenes. This time Ruben throws out a beach ball, a pair of those huge sunglasses without any lenses, an empty egg box, and all kinds of other junk. He comes to Beatrice and Jelly Baby, but he's out of props.

"You can use this," I say. I've got Pen's *Little Trixie* magazine. Maybe I've been reading through some of it, but only because I'm trying to be like Folly and do some research into the Little Trixie world. So far, all I know is that you can make your own doll's clothes out of old socks, and I might have read the comic about Trixie and her pet butterfly, but that counts as research, too.

Beatrice jumps back like I'm handing her a non-speaking part in a second-rate play. "I don't want to use that," she says, and instead of looking angry, she almost looks scared.

Pen is still being a pirate and has that pirate way of looking at things, like she's trying to make one eye do the work of two. She launches herself at the magazine and tears off part of the cover. I don't think she meant to do it. She starts hopping up and down, and Jelly Baby goes after her to calm her down, and Beatrice goes after the *Little Trixie*, like now it's good enough for her to have, and they almost knock heads but Jelly Baby dodges just in time so Beatrice stumbles forward. Jelly Baby puts out her hand to catch

Beatrice but catches the *Little Trixie* instead, and Beatrice lunges at her. Jelly Baby runs, Beatrice follows, around and around the theatre. This is better than that chase sequence we did at the beginning of Act II. I'd sell tickets to this one. Or Folly would sell them and take fifteen per cent of the profits.

"You give that to me!" Beatrice says in short gasps. "If you don't give it here, I'm going to kick that doll of yours in the face the next time I see it!"

You have never seen a hand move as fast as Jelly Baby's. It swings out towards Beatrice, going for her T-shirt. Jelly Baby grabs hold of the ribbon that ties around the back of the shirt and pulls, and the ribbon goes *riiiip* like it's a costume that was made to be torn to pieces onstage. Ruben probably would've told Beatrice to turn around and face away from Jelly Baby, looking kind of towards the audience, and fold her arms and look angry, and that way there wouldn't be a screaming fight. That kind of fight doesn't look as exciting, though, which is why the only kind of fight at the Juicebox involves swords. Well, one sword.

"I'm–" Jelly Baby starts to say something that could be *I'm sorry* and takes off again, but this time Mum blocks her and Jelly Baby thumps into Mum's shoulder. Beatrice skids to a halt kind of like she's on a skateboard, one foot out in front of the other and sideways, which is pretty neat even though I hate to say it.

"Girls, what's the problem?" Mum asks. She looks

from Jelly Baby to Beatrice, and for a second they're just caught in the silence. May's typing something into her phone, Noah's looking at his reflection in the screen of his phone (I only know that because his phone doesn't work), and Pen's trying to dig a hole in the carpet with a stick she got from somewhere.

Mum takes the torn page of the magazine from Jelly Baby and says, "Why do you all want this photograph?"

And this is what happens: a theatre company's complete picture, all at once, for one moment in time.

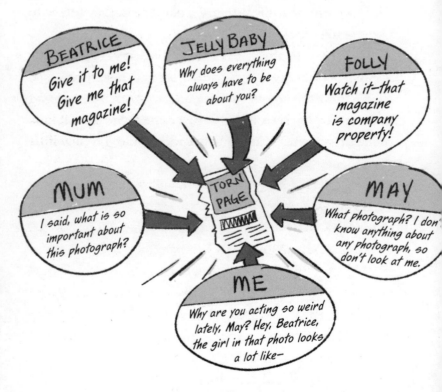

But I don't get to finish my part, because Beatrice does it for me.

"It looks like me, I know. Every stupid month there's a picture of me in that magazine. Me with kittens! Me with a bunch of balloons! Me wearing clown make-up and holding a – a – sock puppet." She glances at Jelly Baby and her cheeks go a fighting kind of red.

"Wow, are you like the official *Little Trixie* model?" Noah asks. "That's cool."

Beatrice gives him a hard look. "Only because my dad makes me. He says if I want to do plays here, then I have to do something for the family business."

The family business? Beatrice's family owns *Little Trixie* magazine? I can see this has made an impression on Folly, too, because he starts messing about with his tie, tapping his fingers on his laptop, anything he can do to make it look like he's paying zero attention to Beatrice and this new little piece of information.

"You're Little Trixie?" I say, and Beatrice glares at me.

This is as good a place as any for the intermission, even if we're only part-way through the second act. You can't tell me I don't know when enough is enough.

INTERMISSION

(Here's what happens during intermission: you get to stand up, stretch your legs, go to the toilet and get a cookie. If I had any meringues, you could have one, but we all know May would bite off my fingers if I tried to take one of hers.)

My brain doesn't stop during intermission. I've got all this bumping around in my brain: Why'd we get all those ledgers and papers? After what Gram and Ruben said, should we buy the karaoke machine? What's happening with all those meringues? Where's Mr Jameson's picture? And bumpiest of all – are we going to make enough money to save the Juicebox Theatre?

Well, I already told you that we do. But at this moment, I don't feel too sure about that.

END
INTERMISSION
(That means get back in your seat.)

When a company gets into a lot of trouble, it can call an emergency meeting where they try to work everything out. Folly calls just such a meeting as soon as Beatrice has sunk down into the only comfortable chair in the Juicebox Theatre and my mum goes to comfort her. "No one calls me Trixie anymore," Beatrice tells her. "I told you, I hate nicknames."

May's gone back to poking at her phone and muttering something about who infested this theatre with a load of hooligans.

"King and Camazzola emergency meeting is called to order."

"Aye," I say. Not because I'm a sailor or a pirate, but because that's what Folly told me to say.

"Sid, you only say that when there's a vote. There's not a vote on calling the meeting to order. I just call it to order. Got it?"

"Aye!" I don't know if that gets a vote or not, but sometimes I just like to mess with Folly. I'm like a puppet: teasing Folly *King*.

Folly doesn't always appreciate it, though. "Anyway, I've been thinking about this whole Beatrice thing, and here's the deal: we're going to do business with the enemy."

If you have to have an enemy, Beatrice is a pretty good one. "But she hates that magazine. Why's she going to buy anything from the Little Trixie Commerce Club?"

Today Folly has on a shirt with a collar. He gives that collar a tug. "She's not buying anything. She's going to be the face of our company, once we get our real stuff to sell."

Look how good I am. I don't say a word about Beatrice's face.

Folly continues. "We just have to come up with our unique selling proposition. What can we offer her that no one else can?"

We could offer her lessons in manners, or maybe a stress ball to squeeze when she gets really upset.

"Think about it: we'll have the real Little Trixie on our advertising campaigns. Who else is going to have that? It's like having Emmit Smith helping you sell your Gators hats down at the pier. I think that girl likes to be in the spotlight, she just doesn't want to do it for the magazine because her dad tells her to. She wants to do it on her own terms. So that's what we'll give her." Folly smiles, and he holds it for a moment, like he's on the cover of a magazine himself. It's not the Classic. It's not the Boy Scout. It's like Folly's swallowed a spotlight. We could light a whole play with his teeth.

"What smile are you doing now, Folly?"

He turns to me, and I can practically feel the heat coming off him. "I call this one Pure Sunshine."

Folly may be what you'd call a seasoned salesman, but he's never reckoned with the likes of the Cockroach before. She's not one of those ladies in the supermarket. When we get close to her and rays of Pure Sunshine start gathering at her feet, she screws up her face and spits, "What do you morons think you're doing? Are you trying to talk to me about the Bible or something, because I've already heard about that."

"What I am trying to talk to you about," Folly says smoothly, "is a veritable bible of consumer products. An opportunity of biblical proportions, you might say. Would you rather be a rich man – excuse me, *lady* – or squeeze through the eye of a needle?"

"That doesn't make any sense," Beatrice points out.

Folly has entered some kind of waking dream, and sense has taken a back seat. "There's sense, and then there's *sense*, am I right? Does it make any sense to turn down a shot at fame and fortune? Because that's what I – that's what *we* – want to give you. My associate here is in town for a photoshoot and he'd like you to be a part of it."

"*In* town? I bet Sid's never *left* this town in his whole life."

That's where she's wrong. I was in Tidewater Beach only two months ago.

"Well, he's here, and he's doing a photoshoot, and we couldn't imagine doing it without you. We want you to be the face of King and Camazzola's Useful Household Products division."

Beatrice's face turns as sour as milk and vinegar. "You're in that stupid club, aren't you? My dad tried to get me to join that, selling junk, but I told him I'd rather die."

You would think Folly's pride would be wounded hearing this, but no. I can see him calling down his personal sales angels as he says, "Beatrice, I'm going to help you out here. Why don't we take a couple of pictures now so you can see what I'm talking about, and when you look them over you can make a decision? Sid, have you got your camera on you?"

Not only do I not have a camera on me, I don't own a camera. I was supposed to get May's old mobile phone when she got a new one, but she can't find it. Pen must have buried it in the woods.

We are in the world of imaginary props here, and I don't think Folly can tell the difference. But it doesn't matter, because Beatrice scoffs. "That's the Puppy Dog close. You give the customer the chance to try something out and hope that they won't be able to resist. That only works on lizard-brains like you."

Folly goes to straighten his bow tie, and it comes off in his hand. He's gone a shade of green he reserves for May, and he gives Beatrice, if I'm not mistaken, the same I'm-going-to-marry-you eyeballs. I hope it's just the bad lighting.

In a low voice, he says, "I can see you're not the average customer, Miss Mountbank. I can see I'm going to have to work a little harder with you. Let's make a list." He gets a notebook out of his briefcase and draws a line down the middle of a blank page. "Let's write down some reasons why you might not want to help us, and some reasons why you should help us. First off–"

Before he can write anything, Beatrice shoots out a loud, "Ha! You're trying the Ben Franklin close on me? Make a list of all the reasons for and against buying something, and make sure the list of reasons *for* is longer than the list against. That's old news. No one uses that strategy anymore. Trust me. I've been around business talk since I was four and a half. My dad has some insane dream that I'm going to take over the business when he retires, so he talks to me about everything."

This is where I think Folly needs a little help. I can only imagine what the sun feels like when it's shining down on glaciers that refuse to melt, but that must be what he's feeling right now. Just the way I do when I'm wrapped up in a banana-yellow curtain dress, I jump in to save the day.

"We have a brand-new strategy we saved for last," I say. "Bet you never heard of this one. Right, Folly?"

Folly only nods, still with his bow tie in his hand.

Beatrice smirks. "Oh, yeah? What is it?"

"It's called the . . . The SWIZ," I say.

"SWIZ?"

"Sure. It's one of those acronym things. Uh, Spit, Wham, Itch, uh, Zing!"

Folly told me once that there's a special deal sales teams make with each other when one of them starts yapping about something that the other one doesn't have a clue about. "You don't say a word unless you know what the deal is," he said. "I learned that one from an informational video about selling property." That video must have made an impression on him, because he lets me go on about the SWIZ like he taught it to me himself. He might get frustrated with me sometimes, but he won't lose his temper. His angel side always wins, which is probably why we're friends, because most of the time mine does too.

I'm using something besides my angel side with Beatrice, though. "It's an advanced strategy, Trixie – I'm sorry, *Beatrice* – so I'm not surprised you don't know about it. It starts with *Spitting* out the truth, which is that personally, I don't care if you want to be in some advertisement for our company or not. We're going to do just fine without you. Probably better, in fact, without your dumb face all over the place."

Whoops. I guess that's the *Wham* part, because Beatrice looks like I just punched her.

142

"But you see," I continue, "it's not just for us that we're trying to make money. It's to keep the Juicebox from having to close forever. Ruben's almost out of money, and he's going to go and paint boat bottoms, and you're not going to have anywhere to satisfy that *Itch* you have to show off anymore, and how are you going to get famous in movies if you can't do that?"

Wait for it: *Zing!*

The light of reason shines in Beatrice's eyes. "I don't know why you're talking about spitting and itching, and I don't like you, but if you have a way to keep this theatre open," she says, "I'm in."

I would stop here for some notes to my actors about that last part, since it was a little bit of a mess. But one of those actors was me, and as you know I'm hopeless at it. Notes wouldn't make a difference. I'd do better listening to Folly go on about business strategy.

He calls it a two-pronged approach. We're going to do our Little Trixie sales and we're going to run these fundraisers and by the end of the summer, the Juicebox will be on solid ground and Folly and his mum will be standing in piles of cash up to their knees. I ask Beatrice why she can't just get the money we need from her dad, and she makes a face.

"Because theatre's not a *viable business model*," she says. "He thinks acting and all that is a waste of time."

"But he bought that balcony for you," I say, even though the memory of it might make her spit at me again.

She doesn't spit. She looks like she might even be too sad to spit. "No, he didn't. I made it myself. That's why it fell apart so easily. But I didn't want you to know that."

I think about Beatrice coming into the theatre when there was no one else around and making her cockroach balcony board by board. There are more kinds of orphans around here than I realized. "It wasn't so bad, you know," I tell her, because I can't stand to be too spiteful to someone whose dad makes her wear clown clothes and I don't know what else, and still has to build her own sets.

"I've made some projections," says Folly, opening up the laptop. He clicks on a file called "Juicebox Income and Expenses".

"Ruben says it costs four thousand dollars to put on a play. That's rent for the theatre, lighting, making the costumes, sets, advertising, all that. He even has to pay for permission to use a script. If the Juicebox does each play six times, that's—"

COST OF PRODUCTION	NUMBER OF PERFORMANCES	BREAK EVEN POINT (PER SHOW)
$4,000.00	6	$666.67

And this time I pay attention. If I'm going to be a director one day, I'd better learn how to Love the Numbers.

"So that break-even point is where we make just enough money to do a show, but we don't have any extra?"

Folly nods. "And Ruben doesn't even get paid unless we make more than that."

I think back to that pitiful stack of dollars Mum put in the cash box after the variety show. Unless each of them was a fifty-dollar bill, we didn't come anywhere close.

"At five bucks a head," Folly says as he plugs some numbers into his spreadsheet, "we'd have to get one hundred and thirteen and a third people here for Amateur Night. That's if we sell a hundred dollars in concessions, which is almost a dollar a person. There are a hundred and fifty seats in the theatre–" *tap, tap,* "which means we have to have a seventy-five point five per cent occupancy rate."

"I bet your dad could pay for a whole year of plays," I tell Beatrice.

She stomps the ground. "I don't think so. He gives ten per cent of his profits to charity every year, but he never gives any to the theatre. Last year he gave five hundred dollars to a charity that takes retired businessmen on rare insect-watching expeditions. He loves insects."

Sounds like a pretty sad excuse for a charity to me.

"Where did he give the rest?" asks Folly.

"That was all. I guess that was ten per cent of whatever his profit was."

"Nope," says Folly. He opens one of the ledgers. "Says here his profit – that's revenue minus expenses – was fifty thousand dollars. Ten per cent of fifty thousand – that's five thousand dollars. If he's giving away five hundred dollars, that's only one per cent of his profit."

"What do you mean, *says here*?" Beatrice muscles her way between us and the ledger, and I mean she muscles, because Folly and I have been so busy building up our brains that we haven't had time to work on our upper body strength training yet. She grabs the book, looks at the cover and reads through some of the pages. "This is all about Little Trixie. Where did you get this?" She slams the ledger down on the laptop's keyboard so hard the loose *F* key pops out and flies away.

I'm waiting for some piece of Zap wisdom to save me from having to tell Beatrice the truth, or at least some outrage from Folly about the expense of repairing office machines, especially when his mum's counting every penny, but Folly just starts wiggling. You might even call it writhing. It's like what a snake might do if it was having a war inside itself, and that war was between keeping its cool and telling you something that would make you swallow your own socks.

Beatrice is not going to be put off by a snake dance. "I could have you thrown in prison and strung up by your ears for larceny," she says.

I don't want to be strung up by my ears for anything, especially for a word that's not in my vocabulary.

Maybe Beatrice hears me thinking this, because she wrinkles her nose at me and says, "That means stealing, Sid. So you'd better tell me just how it happened."

And, to save my ears, I tell her just how it happened.

Beatrice is a good audience. It's like she's acting the part of being an audience, looking right at me and nodding and getting a kind of shocked look on her face.

Folly's still squirming, and finally he bursts out, "I knew there was something funny about it. That's why they packed all the records up and sent them to be destroyed: because Little Trixie is lying about how much money the company makes. Your dad's going to be in trouble, Beatrice. You know what happens when someone lies about how much money they give to charity?"

I shake my head, but Beatrice looks like she knows exactly what happens.

"They go to prison for tax fraud," says Folly. "Just like Al Capone."

Beatrice still looks like she wants to string someone up by their ears, but she just says, "I bet Al Capone would have run a better magazine than *Little Trixie*."

Act II

SCENE FIVE

(Picture a darkened stage with just one light on me, over in the corner.)

I'll just tell you now that I did get out of the Juicebox Theatre alive that day. And I'm happy to say that Jelly Baby helped us make a new *F* key out of black duct tape and white paint, and somehow Folly's mum hasn't noticed it yet.

I'll just tell you also that Noah made the biggest mistake of his life when he said Beatrice should wear her *Little Trixie* clown costume to the Juicebox sometime. She was already mad after finding out that her dad was a liar and a cheat, and the clown costume joke put her over the edge. Maybe I'm going to have to study how to stage a fight, because there seems to be a lot of them going on. This one had kicking, stomping and screaming, and Beatrice was moving so fast it looked like the flying scenes from *Peter Pan*.

But Ruben says the stage does not dwell in the past, so now I'm going to raise the lights and show you what else is going on. We have four spotlights in the Juicebox that we can set up ahead of time to light up a part of the stage, and then Ruben can turn them on and off when he needs them. He writes all the light cues on a lighting schedule, marked *L1*, *L2*, and so on. It looks a lot like one of Folly's spreadsheets. But these I can understand.

Each light will be on just long enough for you to see what's happening, then it goes off. It's more dramatic that way.

L1: There's a tray of meringues on the kitchen table, and there's May in one of Mum's old dressing gowns with her hair pulled back, studying a sheet of music.

L2: There's Jelly Baby in Ruben's living room, making the clown marionette walk up and down.

L3: There's my Gram sitting on the edge of her bed, getting her hair curlicued by Mum, and squeezing her feet into her zebra-striped high heels, which May hates just as much as the orange ones.

L4: There's Beatrice sitting in the middle of a pile of newspaper and glue and paint. Maybe she's posing for some *Little Trixie* craft project. She looks mad enough.

L5: I know I said we only have four spotlights, but

if I had a fifth, I'd put it on Folly, because he's worth watching. Folly is mad. He's pacing back and forth, as much as he can pace in his tiny office, and he's muttering to himself, "You do *not* mess with my momma. You think you can mess with *my* momma? You can*not* mess with *my* momma." Like I said, he's mad. But we don't have time to find out why just yet. You know why?

That's right: it's Amateur Night.

We advertised in the newspaper, we put up posters at Panhandle Pastries, at the Publix and way down at the end of the fishing pier in Blue Crab Bay. Ruben made a poster in Spanish and we took it to the one Mexican restaurant in town.

Beatrice and I even walked through the Casablanca Mall on the Saturday before the show, handing out flyers and trying to look like a worthwhile charitable cause. The mall was mostly empty, and about half of the shops had their metal doors pulled down. A few people took the flyers, but we saw some of them left on benches or thrown away. Beatrice said I should have dressed up like an orphan to make me look more pathetic. I told her she should have dressed like a clown, and then I ran behind a potted palm. But she just said, "Geez, Sid, you think all I do is punch people?"

I don't think that's all she does. But it's what Folly would call a major area of business activity for her.

On the day of the fundraiser, May, Pen, Folly and I

pile into the car with Mum. I call out, "Hey, Dad, can't you just come for a little bit of Amateur Night?"

He already said he couldn't make any of it. He's got some cages to clean at the Pet Palace. I suppose cage-cleaning runs in the family.

He calls back, "Sorry, son! My talent is too amateur even for Amateur Night, but I'll catch you in the morning."

Dad works so hard, I ought to call myself a work orphan. It's not that he never comes to anything at the Juicebox. It's just some times are busier than others. These days he might spend his time painting houses and scooping up poop like I do, but before Mrs Jameson died, he used to go over and listen to her and May singing together all the time. He even took a portable voice recorder with him, because I suppose he thinks May's that good.

That anti-snake prayer Folly and I made up worked so well, I did one for tonight, too – an anti-bad-luck prayer, like this: *Oh Lord, do not let Frankie ruin everything. Oh please, let her stay at home like a good dog and eat Gram's other orange shoe.* Which I half-buried in Folly's garden just by her water bowl, with the heel sticking up attractively.

We are all quiet on the way to the Juicebox. I'm not chattering, May's not telling me to shut up, and even Pen is barely squirming. Folly's clipping and unclipping his bow tie, which he only ever does when he's nervous. After the variety show, we're all wondering how this fundraiser will go.

Even though Folly came up with the idea, he almost didn't come, either. When I told him it was time to go, all he said was, "He can*not* mess with my *momma*."

And for all the times Folly has dragged me back to reality, I do him this favour: I get hold of his bow tie and drag him to the car. "No one's going to mess with your mum. Don't you worry about that."

"*He'd* better worry," says Folly under his breath. "He's trying to mess with my momma."

If you could've seen the ledger Folly was staring at back there during the light cues, you'd have seen a line somewhere among the Little Trixie bookkeeping files that said *Calliope King: $10,500.* If you don't know who Calliope King is, that's because she's got something in common with my dad. She's been hanging around backstage, waiting for her entrance. Calliope King is Folly's mum, and that $10,500 is how much money she invested in Little Trixie.

The part that makes Folly mad, though, is what comes after that, where it says that Calliope King's $10,500 went into some other account called *S.W.I.Z.*, and as far as Folly can tell, after that it disappears. I know Mr Mountbank didn't put that money into South-Western Industrial Zips, since that's just something Jelly Baby made up, but I don't have a clue what actually happened to it, and neither does Folly. When we get to the theatre, it's obvious there's a lot more going on this Thursday night in Hatahatchee than Amateur Night, because the seats aren't exactly filling up. I try to picture Folly's spreadsheet in front of me to work out how much money we're going to make:

NUMBER OF PEOPLE	26, no, 27, 28, 29 – can I count dogs?
DOGS?	Frankie! How'd she get in here?
TOTAL	This is going to be a total catastrophe.

But catastrophe, remember, is the *soul* of theatre, according to Ruben. He says it can mean "disaster" but also in the ancient Greek theatre, it meant "final resolution", and it wouldn't be so bad if we could get to some kind of resolution tonight.

Frankie's slinking around by the stage like she thinks we're doing a revival of Odysseus and Argos, and she's looking for her pile of manure. I point her out to Folly, and he commands her to sit next to him in the concession stand. You might wonder how a dog would get all the way from Hatahatchee Street and find the door of the Juicebox Theatre, but there's a term for that: stage magic. And that's

154

the closest I can come to working out why half the things that happen do.

Mum comes up looking worried. "Have you seen Beatrice? I asked her to be an usher tonight, but I can't find her anywhere."

Have you ever heard that saying about how there are no small parts, only small actors? Well, I don't think Beatrice agrees with that at all. The part of usher is so small, it would make her claustrophobic. But I just tell Mum I haven't seen her anywhere.

Somehow people find their seats without Beatrice's help. Mum's handed them the slips of paper that tell them where they are in the line-up for the evening, and they're waiting for the show to start. I turn down the house lights and everyone goes quiet.

I love it when they do that.

Doña Flor's hosting the show. "Even though she's not an amateur," Jelly Baby said when Ruben asked her to do it, which is true.

Before she took Doña Flor out of her case, I asked Jelly Baby if she was scared that Beatrice was going to kick her in the face. Jelly Baby said, "I told you, I'm not worried about Beatrice. She can't kick high enough. And Doña Flor likes to be out. She doesn't want to stay locked up in a box all the time."

Like at the variety show, Jelly Baby gets Amateur Night started with a dance. She goes all the way from the back of the theatre down the centre aisle and onto the stage, and

Doña Flor's nodding at people with that smile of hers the whole way. I can just about hear some of them thinking, *How am I, with my amateur performance, going to beat that?*

When the music dies down and the clapping is over, Jelly Baby says, "Welcome to Amateur Night. Bienvenidos. Tonight we give the stage to you. First up: Esther Marie Quant, the Juggling Dynamo!"

The Juggling Dynamo turns out to be no bigger than me and about eighty years older. You've never seen juggling till you've seen someone throwing six kinds of fruit in a circle over their head. Jelly Baby and Doña Flor come out afterwards to get the audience clapping and introduce the next performer, and I'm clapping like crazy for Esther Marie Quant.

After that, though, I'll be honest: it all kind of goes downhill. Someone sings "This Land Is Your Land", and then the next person goes up looking kind of embarrassed and sings "This Land Is Your Land", and then the next three people pass on their turns. I just about lose interest and hope altogether and then a kid I recognize from school tries breakdancing and one of his shoes flies up into the air and lands on his head. At that point, Jelly Baby calls intermission and Ruben comes out to give the kid an ice pack.

A few people buy snacks, and it's only then that I see the gaping hole on the table where May's meringues used to be, and a trail of crumbs leading towards the door.

There's a thing in plays where important events repeat themselves for emphasis. It's supposed to help the audience pay attention. Well, I don't know why this is worth paying any attention to, but you might as well remember it. A memory of those meringues is all we've got, anyway.

I wish Francolina had sniffed out that dirty old meringue thief, but she's been too busy trying to get herself back onstage. "Do you have anything we can tie her up with?" I ask Folly after I sell a Hog Farmer to the unsuspecting Dynamo.

"Sometimes I wish I could just call Zap Zapter and ask him a question," says Folly, who's not thinking about the Frankie problem at all. And I don't blame him.

"What do you think Zap would say about this?"

"Zap would say you can't let a Fool make you a Tool, but Beatrice's dad did make a tool out of my mum. And me. I still don't have a strategy for this, and I've read all Zap's books."

I feel that I'm being called on to give some guidance to a friend in need, but I don't have a strategy, either. The only strategy I know is the one I made up, and I can tell Folly's not in the mood for any talk about spitting and itching. So I make a modification: "Stick With It, Zap Junior," I say.

"Stick with what?"

"The script."

Folly picks up a cookie and takes a bite out of it, which shows how upset he is, to be eating his stock. "But I don't have a script, Sid. That's the problem."

I take the rest of the cookie out of Folly's hand and eat it myself, to save his conscience, and I say, "Then I'll have to help you write one."

"Stick With It, huh?" he says. "I'll stick with it. I'm going to work out what's going on at Little Trixie, starting with their accounts, and I'm going to make Beatrice's dad tell me why he's cheating people."

He's cheating the Juicebox, too, if you think about it. If Beatrice's dad was honest about how much money he had to give away, he could give some of it to us. Who says we're not a viable business model? "We should tell him he has to pay us if he wants all those records back," I say. "Otherwise we'll call the police, and he'll probably go to prison."

Folly grows about a foot when I say that. "Sid, that's extortion. You never, never, never make someone pay with a threat like that. *You* could go to prison. That's not how we operate at King and Camazzola."

"How do we operate?"

"With decency and dignity and respect for our fellow man, even if our fellow man is kind of a scuzzball. It's pretty much standard to do that."

I know how much money you can get operating that way, but I'll go along with it anyway.

I'm just about to say that maybe Beatrice's dad would *volunteer* to pay up and then it wouldn't be extortion, when the house lights dim again and people take their seats for Amateur Night's second act.

Jelly Baby's back onstage introducing the next act. I wonder if it's tough for Jelly Baby under that puppet get-up. Does it hurt her head to have the helmet clamped on like that? I have a feeling she'd do it no matter how big a pain it was because she and Doña Flor together are something else, and she knows it.

Speaking of something else, the next act is wobbling its way up to the stage, and I'm having trouble working out just what it is. It's almost like the first time I saw Doña Flor, but that was like having a piece of art looming over you. This thing has got a cylinder for a head, with giant eyes and a gaping hole painted bright red that might be its mouth, skinny arms and a pair of legs that end in bright orange trainers.

It's not until I see movement out of the corner of my eye that I realize Folly's left the concession stand and looks like he's trying to army crawl his way down the aisle. There's only one thing that will make Folly do something so undignified, and that thing is Frankie.

Frankie's sniffing her way down the centre aisle ahead of Folly, heading towards that pair of orange trainers like she's after a couple of barbecued chickens. What is it with that dog and orange shoes? I didn't think dogs could even see orange. Maybe she can smell it. A few people turn their heads to Folly, but he puts a finger to his lips like he's on special ops duty and keeps going.

The strange creature makes it up the steps at the side of the stage and wobbles over to Jelly Baby, who's saying, "Please put your hands together for Madame Pinkola Swizarola, who–" She breaks off when she sees the thing coming across the stage. "Who–"

Whatever it is Madame Pinkola Swizarola's supposed to be doing, Jelly Baby can't say it. She can only stand there with Doña Flor's big smiling head smiling away and pretend like whatever's about to happen is going to be fantastic.

The look painted onto Madame's face reminds me of something. It seems to be saying, *Just you try and get me off this stage, Sid.*

It takes me two seconds to realize what's happened. It flashes through my mind like a montage: there's Beatrice with all that newspaper, making a big head and painting big red cockroach lips on it, there she is signing up for Amateur Night, and now there she is heading straight for Jelly Baby, and I can only think that she disguised herself because she means to keep her promise to kick Doña Flor in the face since she hates puppets so much.

I don't know if Ruben understands what's about to happen, and I don't have time to wait. I'm going to save

Doña Flor. She survived the first attempt on her life, and she'll survive this one, too.

The fastest way to go would be to run down the centre aisle, too, but it's too full of Frankie and Folly, so I head down the side aisle. The stage is low enough that I can jump right up there and grab Doña Flor out of the way. The thing is, I can't just scoop up Doña Flor and carry her to safety, because she's tied to Jelly Baby. Jelly Baby's four inches taller than I am, and Doña Flor's even taller than that.

Instead, it happens like this: I'm running, and Folly starts running, and Beatrice/Madame Pinkola Swizarola is still bearing down on Jelly Baby. Both Beatrice and Jelly Baby get startled when they hear us coming and start to keel over. Frankie takes a dive for the orange trainers and Folly goes after her but overshoots, and he leaps into the air like a great blue heron taking off. Also like a great blue heron taking off, I leap into the air to save Jelly Baby, but Folly tackles me. And just like in one of those Venn diagrams that Folly likes so much, there we all are in almost the same place at the same time. I take Folly's bow tie to the eye, bounce off of Madame Pinkola Swizarola, and we fall to the stage like the amateurs we are.

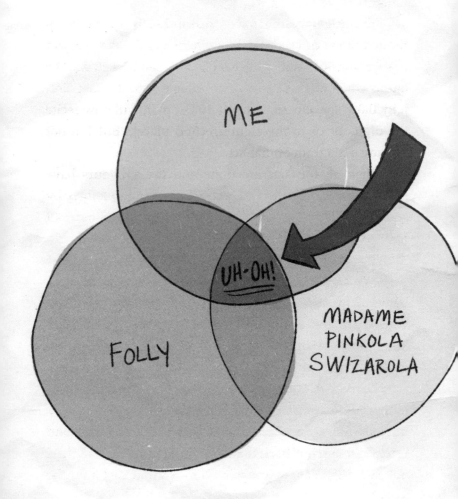

It's as close as we're going to get to the soul of theatre tonight.

I'm going to hand it to Beatrice and Folly: they pick up the wreckage of Madame Pinkola Swizarola and one sad orange dog without a word and carry it all backstage. The audience is laughing, like that was just another act, and Jelly Baby announces, "Mr Vitaly Dropkin will now recite the digits of pi to the eighty-second place!" But I'm not making a diagram of that act.

When all the acts are done and the amateurs have shuffled out of the Juicebox, I go backstage with Jelly Baby and help put Doña Flor back in her case. Which means I help her get out from underneath Doña Flor.

There is a way to do everything, I suppose, and the way to get Jelly Baby out of Doña Flor seems like a cross between gymnastics and magic until I'm standing there with a papier-mâché head resting on my arms and Jelly Baby is folding up all Doña Flor's insides to put her away for the night.

"Beatrice isn't crazy," I say, even though Beatrice isn't doing a very good job of backing me up on that.

Jelly Baby gets Doña Flor all settled in her case and I help her carry it back upstairs. She says, "I know she's not crazy. She believes in something. I know just how she feels."

"But you got into that fight with her at theatre camp."

Jelly Baby laughs like she's trying not to laugh. "That

163

fight? That was so fake. At least, *I* was acting. Teasing the king, remember?" She holds up a hand like it's got a hand puppet on it and pretends to bite me on the arm.

We go back downstairs. In one of the dressing rooms, Beatrice pulls a slab of putty off her nose with a sour old look.

"First it's your dog that ruins everything, now it's you. You want to help the Juicebox Theatre? Maybe you should get as far away from it as you can." There's still some putty at the sides of her nose, like some kind of nose disease. Mum offered to help clean her face up, but Beatrice wasn't having any of it.

"Why are you wearing face goo under that thing?" I ask. "No one could see it was you. I mean, I could, but I have better eyes than most people."

"Your eyes . . . your eyes aren't any better . . ." I can tell she's too angry and sad to finish her insult. "I just thought if anyone saw me under here, maybe they wouldn't know it was me. It would be embarrassing."

"What is that thing, anyway?" I ask. "You look like one of those dancing soup tins from TV."

Jelly Baby says, "It's not that bad. You did a pretty good job," at the same time that Beatrice says, "Yeah, well, her puppet looks like a big old stupid tomato in a yellow dress." And then she goes as red as a big old stupid tomato.

"Why were you sneaking up on Jelly Baby?" I ask. "What were you going to do to her?"

Beatrice's glare stabs me like a pitchfork, but the look she gives Jelly Baby is a little less sharp. "I wasn't sneaking anywhere. I *was* the next act. I had a whole routine I was going to do. You can think that's stupid, but I don't care."

Funny as it is, I don't think it's stupid. I think the nose putty is stupid, but I think Jelly Baby's right: Beatrice believes in this old theatre like I do, and she can't stand to see other people light it up and not be there herself, too. She didn't disguise herself to ruin Doña Flor, she disguised herself to try to *be* Doña Flor.

"You can't compete with Jelly Baby," I say. "She's a professional."

"So am I!" And I see right down to that blue flame that burns at Beatrice's insides, making it so she can't sit still and watch. If Jelly Baby has a giant puppet, then she has to have one, too. Even if hers is nowhere near as good. It's sitting in the corner now, right where Beatrice threw it, and I can see it's just hollow. It doesn't have any of Doña Flor's bones, the sticks and mechanisms inside her that make her seem alive.

And I want to forget that Beatrice tried to show up Jelly Baby and nearly ruined Doña Flor by falling over on top of her. I want to tell her that all she has to do is ask for help and a hundred people would help her, but Jelly Baby sits down next to Beatrice and starts talking to her and then Folly comes in and calls an emergency meeting.

"And don't say 'aye'," he says to me. "We have to find

out who's stealing the meringues. Every time, our revenue decreases by–"

But I don't even

let Folly get started

on that.

"Believe me," I say, "I'm going to track that thief down. I already saw a trail of crumbs, which I'm going to follow as soon as I tell Beatrice there's still a chunk of crud on her face."

Beatrice looks in the mirror and scrapes the rest of the putty off her nose, bouncing one of her ugly looks at me and pinching her lips together.

"Who cares about following trails of crumbs?" she says. "I'd rather talk about revenue. Or puppets." She leans on the dressing table and sulks, which shows just how much she cares about revenue at this moment, but Folly doesn't see that part.

"Well, if you want to talk about revenue–"

Jelly Baby says, "If you want to talk about puppets–"

And I leave them to it.

Unfortunately, I walk right into another discussion of revenue. What happens next is like the scene back there where we counted the money from the variety show and we all had sad faces about it afterwards. I'm not doing that again, since you already know what that looks like. I'll just say that Amateur Night was not the success we hoped it would be, and summer is coming to an end in Hatahatchee without any good prospects for the old Juicebox Theatre. I'm saying extortion might be the way to go.

Act III
SCENE ONE

(Back in the toolshed.

This is where I said I'd put in a thunderstorm, but now I don't know. I'm thinking we might need a whole hurricane to make the point. And I don't know how to do hurricanes yet.)

Cue a couple of happy summer crickets chirping, and my dad whistling. He's painting all the windowsills on Folly's house, but you can't see him because he's at the front and we're at the back, squeezed together in the toolshed, which is now the Boardroom. That's where big business meetings happen.

We have done the unthinkable. We have let Beatrice in.

But we've let Jelly Baby in, too, and explained everything to her, so that makes up for it. Whatever she and Beatrice talked about after Amateur Night, it looks like they've worked out how to be friendly, even if they're not exactly friends.

"I've been inside a boardroom before, and it did not look like this." Beatrice swats at a spider's web, one of the ones we hung up on purpose to keep the likes of Pen out of the toolshed. "Can't we go somewhere clean?"

"We're an entrepreneurial start-up," Folly tells her. "You start in a garage or a shed and move up when you hit the big time. Zap Zapter—"

It's not my place to interrupt the words of the great Zap Zapter, except we're in kind of a hurry here. Mum and Ruben decided to have one last big fundraiser for the theatre: a charity auction. They think people might bid high out of sympathy. We've already gone around getting donations from businesses all over Hatahatchee. Mr Jameson even donated a whole website design. I say, "Either we have to make enough money with the auction, or we have to get it out of your dad without going to prison for extortion. I bet he'd give us a lot of money if we told him what we know, but I don't want to end up in prison. For extortion," I repeat, in case she missed it.

"So what you're telling me," Beatrice says when I'm done, "is that you don't want to go to prison for extortion."

"Right."

"But you want to get money out of my dad."

"Right."

"In exchange for incriminating evidence."

"Right!" She's got it now.

"I think you have a problem, then."

"The problem is that Sid doesn't understand the subtlety of the enterprise," Folly says over my head in his Zap Junior voice. "But I know that you do, Beatrice, because you are, after all, in sales."

She huffs. "*I* am an artist."

Zap Junior says, "I think of myself the same way. When I make a good sales pitch, that's an art. So we're speaking the same language. What we need to do is find our unique selling proposition."

"What we need to do," I say, "is find your dad's motivation."

"What we need to do," says Beatrice, "is find his weak spot. And he's got a couple of them."

It's sad that Beatrice knows that right off.

Folly uncovers one of the Little Trixie boxes, and Beatrice flinches, but maybe that's just because a bad illustration of her own goofy poofball head is smiling up at her. She looks at the shipping label and the packing list inside the box.

"Look here. It says Shred King Data Destruction on the packing list," she says. "But the shipping label on the box says Folly King. I bet he was trying to print a label for Shred King, but he clicked on the wrong name in his database. He's never been good at using computers." She sighs. "So he knew he had to get rid of the evidence, but he totally messed up how to do it. Laziness is one of his weak spots. He should have double-checked. And why would he ship records off to be destroyed in a box that says Little Trixie all over it? Isn't the whole point of destroying stuff that no one ever finds out you did something wrong?"

I can see Beatrice giving her dad a lecture on how to be a better criminal. It's like a part you're playing, and no one's going to believe you if you don't throw your whole self into it.

"Can we tell him that we'll give him the records if he bids on something big at the auction?" I say. "Then he wouldn't be giving any money directly to us."

"That just sounds like some fancy type of extortion," says Folly.

"He wouldn't come to any fundraiser for the theatre, anyway," Beatrice says. "He wouldn't waste his money."

"Does he ever come to your shows?" I ask.

Beatrice flicks a spider off her arm. "No. Not even when I have a major role. Not even when I play a cockroach, and insects are like his favourite thing next to counting his money. You know what his dream is? He wants to go down to south Florida and start this Sweet Water Insect Zoo. That's what he cares about. He doesn't care what I do."

I guess that's another one of his weak spots.

"Sweet Water Insect Zoo–?" Folly starts to say, but then Jelly Baby speaks up. She's been quiet up to now, listening to all this, but I suspect she sees we're not really getting anywhere.

"What if we make him bid *on* the ledgers? If he knows they're up for auction, he won't care how much it costs him to get them back. We don't even have to say we know what's in there. As far as we know, it's just some ledgers and office supplies."

"That's a great idea," says Beatrice, like she's surprised to hear herself say it.

Folly's getting that gaga look again, and when Jelly Baby adds, "We could even set up a false bidder to push up the price," I swear I can see his heart beating right out of his shirt.

"Sid, you could bid against him," Beatrice says. "It'll make him crazy that a kid is trying to show him up."

"I wouldn't be any good at that," I say. "But my Gram would do it. I know she would. Hey, we should write all this down, like in a script. I told you I'd help you write one, Folly. We can plan the whole thing out."

"If only it was as easy as following a script," Beatrice sighs.

If only.

Sidney Horatio Camazzola presents

SAVE THE JUICEBOX!

CAST OF CHARACTERS

THE SWAN .... Beatrice Mountbank

THE GREEDY RICH GUY .... Jefferson Mountbank

THE AUCTIONEER .... Ruben Aparicio

THE BIG SHOT .... Mr DeVaughan Jameson

THE DEAD DOG .... Francolina King

THE KARAOKE KING .... Hank Camazzola

With a guest appearance by

Madame Pinkola Swizarola as *Herself*

Directed by Sidney Horatio Camazzola

Sponsor:

Panhandle Pastries

Time for a cookie, cookie!

Owner and operator:

Miss Alabama Harper

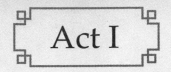

Act I

(The Mountbank home. THE SWAN is at her
father's feet, pleading.)

THE SWAN

Oh, you must come to the theatre, Father
dear! You simply must!

THE GREEDY RICH GUY

Never! The theatre is not a viable
business model!

THE SWAN

It is too a viable business model!

THE GREEDY RICH GUY

I'll never set foot in that theatre!

THE SWAN
(sobbing)

But what if I told you it could save
. . . your life!

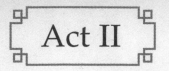

Act II

(A fancy auction house.)

THE AUCTIONEER

For this lot of eight boxes of used ledgers,
I have nine thousand six hundred dollars! Do
I hear nine thousand six hundred and one?

THE BIG SHOT

Nine thousand six hundred and one!

THE GREEDY RICH GUY

Nine thousand six hundred and two!

THE BIG SHOT

Ten thousand!

THE GREEDY RICH GUY

Oh, no! Alas! I do not have enough money to
buy my freedom! My shame will spread across
this earth and my daughter will never be
allowed in a theatre again due to my own
greed and selfishness and the fact that I
am a scuzzball!

THE SWAN

(sobbing)

Oh, Father!

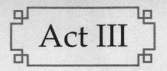

Act III

(THE GREEDY RICH GUY is asleep, and
MADAME PINKOLA comes to him in a dream.
Or is it a dream?

P.S. There is a hurricane.)

MADAME PINKOLA

Woo-ooo-ooo!

THE GREEDY RICH GUY

(shivering, teeth chattering)

Who—who's there?

MADAME PINKOLA

I am the spirit of the Juicebox Theatre,
and you have killed me!

(lightning flashes)

THE GREEDY RICH GUY

No! I'm not a murderer!

MADAME PINKOLA

Then what's this dead dog doing on your
bedroom floor?

(points to THE DEAD DOG, lying dead in
the middle of the floor with her tongue
hanging out)

(Thunder crashes. THE KARAOKE KING
appears upstage left and starts singing
"If I Were a Rich Man" from Fiddler on
the Roof.)

THE GREEDY RICH GUY

No! How can I make up for all my sins and
misdeeds?

MADAME PINKOLA

You will give your money to the Juicebox
Theatre so that it can live again!

THE GREEDY RICH GUY

(sobbing)

Okay! I will!

THE DEAD DOG
Woof!

Applause, applause, and everyone takes a bow. The
Juicebox is back on its feet, Folly's mum gets a nice cheque
from Beatrice's dad, and everyone wins.

And that's how it's going to be.

Act III

SCENE TWO

(I'm sorry to say this, but we're in the bathroom at my house. Only some serious internal motivation could get me inside a bathroom with May. I need her help.)

"It's not going to be like that at all, Sid," May says after I act all the parts out for her. She's staring at herself in the mirror, trying on six different kinds of lipstick. "I wouldn't be part of any scheme you come up with. You're too melodramatic."

"This is theatre," I say. "It's good to be dramatic." May just rolls her eyes, which is funny because if we were onstage, you wouldn't be able to see it. "And anyway, April-May-June, I don't hear you coming up with any great ideas to raise money for the Juicebox."

"We could get your dignity out of the rubbish and sell it," she says through tight lips. "Although I don't think anyone would pay very much for it. It's so small."

"But your meringues are small, and you sell them," I say, and I get ready for May to take a swing at me. But she goes completely still. Her hand holding the lipstick freezes in mid-air and she catches my eye in the mirror.

No spotlight is shining on me, but I'm starting to sweat. "I know you do," I say. "I saw one at Mr Jameson's house."

"Maybe I gave him one." She moves a step closer to me. I back away one step, but it's a small bathroom, and May's between me and the door.

"It was in a box with some of Miss Alabama Harper's cookies. Mr Jameson was trying to write a description of it for her website."

"'The Cookie of the Heavens' is what it's supposed to be called," May says, looking far away for a moment. "'Lighter than air, sweeter than angels.' I told her that." Then she remembers who she's mad at. "Don't you ever learn not to poke your nose over other people's fences? I make them, I sell them, and it has nothing to do with you."

"I get you the eggs," I say.

I jump back before May's long fingers can get a firm grip on my earlobe. "It's not a crime to sell meringues online. As it happens, people like them. I can't make them fast enough. I even had to go in there and get some of those eggs myself."

"Aha! That's how you got that scratch on your arm."

May sniffs. "That delinquent rooster."

Then she grabs for my arm. May doesn't do anything gently. "Sidney – Sid – don't tell. Please? It's not really stealing, right? I don't want to get excluded from the theatre or something. I'll never do *Evita*. I'll never have a stage career. My life," she says as she tightens her grip on my arm and gives a twist, "is in your hands."

Maybe so, but it feels more like the other way around. "Just let go," I groan. "And say you'll help us out."

May does one final yank on my poor practically broken arm. "I'll help you out, you snot-wad," she says, giving me a shove. "Only because I love the theatre."

Part 2

So I got that mystery all sorted out. Well, mostly sorted out. They ought to hire me down at the Hatahatchee Police Department. But I don't want to join the police. I have a serious theatrical production to get on with. I'm going to call it:

HOW TO STAGE A CATASTROPHE

CAST OF CHARACTERS

BEATRICE...Beatrice Mountbank

VOICE OF THE PRESIDENT OF THE HATAHATCHEE
CHAMBER OF COMMERCE / VOICE OF ZAP ZAPTER
....Folly King

~~THE KARAOKE QUEEN~~...............................~~Vee Christensen~~

~~A PAIN~~ THE KARAOKE QUEEN..................May Camazzola

THE JUICEBOXER..................................Penelope Camazzola

THE GHOST.........................Tamara Christensen Camazzola

ARGOS..Francolina King

THE CRESTFALLEN PUPPETEER........Juliana "Jelly Baby"
Aparicio

THE HELPFUL NEIGHBOUR........Mr DeVaughan Jameson

YOU DON'T MESS WITH.........................Mrs Calliope King

And

In his first major role in front of the curtain
(Ever)

THE ORPHAN BOY....................Sidney Horatio Camazzola

Directed by Sidney Horatio Camazzola, in part.
The other part is just how it all happened.

Act I

SCENE ONE

(In Beatrice's house.

I'm not sticking with real script format here, even though May said it's getting confusing. But things are happening fast, and I have a feeling we're going to get off script anyway. So I'm just going to keep up as best I can. So there, May.)

Mr Mountbank is at home, counting his piles of money. All across his face it's written, *I cheated and I got away with it! Nobody's ever going to find out, because I destroyed the evidence!* The phone rings.

"Little Trixie Nationwide Enterprises," he says. He fumbles with the speakerphone, and holds the phone out in front of him because he's way too important to hold a phone up to his own head.

"Mr Jefferson Mountbank, this is the President of the Hatahatchee Chamber of Commerce. The reason I'm calling–"

"Sir, what an honour!" Mr Mountbank starts to rub the side of his face kind of nervously. "Of course, when I quoted you in the article I wrote for *Western Florida Businessman's Quarterly*, I – I told them I was using some of your words, but they must have forgotten to say that, ha ha."

"I'm not calling about that," says the President smoothly. "That's small potatoes to me, you understand. No, I'm calling about something quite different. I'm a charitable man, Mr Mountbank, as I know you are yourself."

The President pauses for Mr Mountbank to agree, which takes him a second. "Oh, sure, sure. Always giving money away! Can hardly keep the stuff in my pockets!"

"That's good to hear. I always say money grows the more you spread it around."

"That's a good one! I'll make a note of that." Mr Mountbank is not making a note.

"Well, I am organizing a little fundraiser for a local institution that I understand you are acquainted with. I'm holding an auction for the Juicebox Theatre. It's for charity, as I said, and I'm inviting only the high society of Hatahatchee to attend. It's a simple idea: you'll come to the auction and bid on whatever strikes your fancy. Bid high, because all the money goes to charity, like I said."

"What if nothing strikes my fancy?"

"Oh, I bet something will stick out to you. Besides, you love giving money away, so even if you don't like anything in particular, just bid anyway. It's for charity."

"It's for charity," repeats Mr Mountbank, but he doesn't sound too excited.

"That's right. I'll expect to see you there at six p.m. on the day of the auction."

"I'll be there!" Mr Mountbank declares. He's just standing still now, waiting for more wisdom to come to him, but the President hangs up.

Over at my house, Folly puts the phone down and smiles at his own performance.

"That was pretty good, Folly," I say. "And you say you don't act."

Act I

SCENE TWO

(I don't know if Scene Two gets a setting. Think of it more like a voiceover.)

Scene Two has a bunch of stuff where Mr Mountbank brags to some of his business acquaintances about how he's got a special invitation from the President of the Hatahatchee Chamber of Commerce and he's going to some high-society charity auction and that he's going to find a way to pay less than anyone else there and walk out with the best prize. I'm not going to play it out for you, because when we were all back in the Boardroom and Beatrice was telling us about it, I almost puked. I must have made an awful noise, because Mr Jameson, who was on his back patio, asked if everything was all right.

But it's an important scene, because remember what Mr Jameson said all that long time ago about what happens when you've been thinking too highly of yourself?

SCENE THREE

(Back on Hatahatchee Street. What I like about Hatahatchee Street is you can see all the way from my house to Mr Jameson's to Folly's on one little stage. So we can go from one to the other without too much trouble.)

This auction has to go just right. Maybe we can't really fill the theatre with the high society of Hatahatchee, if there even is any, but we can get out some costumes from when the seven-to-nines did a Fancy Nancy play, and maybe borrow some clothes from Gram. I'm not going to ask Folly to pretend to be the President in person, because there are about seven reasons why that wouldn't work.

Two weeks before the auction, I'm sitting eating cornflakes with Mr Jameson on his porch. I've cleaned out the coop, and Folly's off selling eggs.

"Question time," says Mr Jameson.

I want to ask if he can see into the future, if he can promise everything's going to work out just fine. I want to ask if he has four thousand dollars he can give the Juicebox and then I wouldn't have to worry about the auction. But before I open my mouth, he goes on, "That is, I have a question for you."

"Oh," I say. "Well, you have unlimited question privileges with me."

"Did you know that I won an award for my web design company?"

I'll admit, I was hoping his question would be more along the lines of, *Can I give you four thousand dollars cash right now?* But I try not to look disappointed as I say, "No, I didn't know that."

"Well, I did," says Mr Jameson. "It's a pretty sweet award, too. It's always brought me luck, and I remember you saying you could use a bit of luck a while ago."

"You are above average," I say.

He unzips the pouch that's strapped to one of the arms of his chair and takes out a small plastic case with a handle. "Sometimes, Sid, when magic isn't available to us, luck and a little strategy is the next best thing. So I want you to take this."

He hands me the case.

"What's the strategy?"

"The strategy is, open in the event of emergency only."

"What is it?" I'm hoping it's a bayonet or something I can use to keep Mr Mountbank in line, but I know the case is too small.

"You'll just have to wait and see."

"How will I know when to open the case?"

"You'll know."

"I thought you said I had unlimited question privileges."

"Even unlimited has its limits, Sid."

* * *

That afternoon, Mum drives me and Folly into Hatahatchee, and we go to Panhandle Pastries to ask Miss Alabama Harper to come to the auction. Since she's a theatre kid from way back, I tell her the whole deal. I know I can trust her with our plans.

"Jefferson Mountbank, huh?" she says. "He never was nice to me when we were at school. I paid him for a yearbook, and he gave me a photo album with a bunch of pictures of himself. I still haven't forgiven him. I'm in."

Of course all the kids are in already, so when we're done at Panhandle Pastries and we head over to the Juicebox to check in with Ruben, everyone just spends their time picking the best costumes. Pen wants to wear her pirate patch with her pink fairy dress, and I say the pirate patch is a giveaway that we're not really high society. She steps on my foot.

Ruben asks us if we should provide some kind of entertainment at the start of the auction, in case it brings more people in. Jelly Baby has an idea to tell a story with Doña Flor about generosity. "To soften Beatrice's dad up, you know, before he has to open his wallet."

"Or shame him," says Beatrice with a grin wider than a hippopotamus.

Folly's throwing a pen in the air and catching it, like he's paying no attention to us, but then he says, "He's not going to listen to any story about generosity. You need to come across strong. I'm recommending the Hamlet close."

"*Hamlet?*" says Beatrice. "That's not a sales strategy, that's a play."

"It's a strategy, too," says Folly. "Hamlet is just like you lot. He wants to get his uncle to confess to killing his dad – Hamlet's dad, that is, who was the king – so he puts on a play where the king's brother kills him and becomes king himself, and he watches how his uncle reacts. His uncle can't watch it because he feels so bad, Hamlet knows he's guilty, bam."

"When did you read *Hamlet?*" I ask.

"I didn't," says Folly. "I just read about it in one of Zap's books. He did something like that once to catch one of his business partners, because he was being dishonest."

"Did it work?"

"I don't know how it worked for Zap Zapter," says Beatrice, "but in *Hamlet*, everyone dies at the end. Still," she shrugs, "let's give it a try."

"Give what a try?" says Mum, coming over with a load of old costumes she's going to fix up. I don't say anything about our plans to Mum, because she would only try to talk to me about my conscience like she always does, and I don't care what Beatrice says about *Hamlet*. My conscience feels just fine.

SCENE ONE

(Remember, this is where
I said sometimes you run
into problems.)

(My house. In the kitchen, because it's too late to make a new set.)

I think everything is in place. Beatrice's dad is coming to the auction, and Folly's going to get the eight Little Trixie boxes down there. Everything's going to be sitting out at the start of the auction, so Mr Mountbank will see what's there. He'll know what's in those boxes, and he'll bid on them if he wants to save himself from prison.

Ruben is going to be the auctioneer. We're telling him half the truth: we're donating a bunch of office supplies, and we're asking him to start bids at $500. And I have a secret weapon. Pen's going to be sitting there with a bottle of juice, and if anyone besides Mr Mountbank or Gram starts bidding, she's going to spill it in their lap. They'll have to get up and clean themselves off, and by then the whole thing will be over.

I catch Gram first thing in the morning a couple of days before the auction. She'd been lying low in bed for a little while, so I thought I'd do something nice for her. And that always makes it easier to ask for something in return.

"I washed your spangle sweater, Gram," I say, handing it to her along with a cup of coffee.

"Oh, you know the way straight to a Danish grandma's heart, don't you?"

She's only part Danish and she was born in Chattanooga, but I know better than to correct someone when I have a favour to ask.

"I do know the way," I say. "But it's hard to miss your heart, since it's so large and generous." I try the Boy Scout for emphasis. Eyes open wider than normal, but not too wide.

"And I know what it looks like when someone's trying to butter me up, my bug-eyed grandson," says Gram. "There's so much butter in here, I could slip if I was standing up. So why don't you tell me what it is you're hoping I'll say yes to."

I drop the Boy Scout and tell her all about Mr Mountbank and the auction, and how we need someone to be the false bidder. I add that if that someone wore glamorous clothes and had a choice of eight different hairstyles, it would be even better.

I thought I'd have to spread a little more butter around, but right away she cries, "I wouldn't miss a chance to help your theatre, Sid. I have always wanted one of my grandchildren to follow me in the performing arts, and I couldn't be more proud of you."

"But May and Pen are both in the theatre, too. And I'm not onstage ever, like you were. I mostly do props."

"True, but you have a real feel for it, Sid. With you, it's true love. I don't know if Pen will ever say a word onstage, and May is too afraid of making a fool of herself. I said I wanted someone to follow *me* in the performing arts, someone brave enough to know that sometimes you have to make a fool of yourself. That someone, my dear boy, is you."

Which is a compliment, I think.

Act II

SCENE TWO

There are two things to know about Scene Two. First, a week before the auction, Jelly Baby's dad has told her to come home. She's supposed to leave the night of the auction, which means Doña Flor has to be packed up and shipped, too. I only hope she doesn't have to leave until the auction's over, because I know she thinks of the Juicebox like we all do, like it belongs to us, and she cares what happens just as much as we do. She's even going to tell her dad she wants to come up here every summer, which is all right with me.

The second part happens when Beatrice walks up to us the next day at the Juicebox and says, "My dad's not coming to the auction. He's going to Miami on business."

(The setting for all that was the Juicebox, by the way. I'm going too fast for my own good.)

Act III

SCENE ONE

(We're in Folly's den. I wasn't expecting that, so if some of the furniture looks like it belongs in my kitchen or Ruben's apartment, well, we're being thrifty.)

If we don't have Mr Mountbank at the auction, we might as well hang up a CLOSED sign on the doors of the Juicebox Theatre. Other people might come and bid on things, but that won't get us near what we need for a whole season of plays. We have another strategy session, this time in Folly's den. My dad's in the toolshed – cue the sound of power tools.

Jelly Baby must be interested in power tools, because she watches my dad for a minute, then comes into our meeting looking just like Folly does when he's got an idea to chew on.

"Isn't there some way you can make your dad go later?" she asks Beatrice. "He has to be here for Saturday."

Beatrice shakes her head. "He says it's a make-or-break trip. Even the President of the Hatahatchee Chamber of Commerce isn't important enough to make him change his mind. My mum is going, too, because she does all the marketing. They tried to drag me along, but I said the auction was too important, and no way am I going to stand around holding poodle puppies like an idiot when my theatre needs me. Besides, it's not even for *Little* . . . for the magazine."

"What's the purpose of this business trip?" Folly asks.

"He's meeting with some new investors for this insect zoo he wants to start."

"Investors," says Folly, rubbing his hands together. That's not because of a bad stage direction from me – he came up with that himself, looking like a GREEDY RICH GUY would. "Maybe he won't need to go to Miami to meet investors if he's got a big one right here at home."

"Like who?" He's not going to get Mr Jameson or Miss Alabama Harper to become a major investor in an insect museum, even if Miss Alabama does make Squashed Bug cookies.

"Like Zap Zapter."

"How are you going to get him to come?" I ask. "I bet

he's never even been to Hatahatchee. He wouldn't come just because a couple of kids asked him to."

Folly raises his eyebrows a couple of times at me. That would also be a bad stage direction, but again, it's not my fault. "Oh, he might come. He just might."

"No, he wouldn't–" I start to say. And then I get it.

Act III

SCENE TWO

(Back at Beatrice's house.)

Mr Mountbank is packing a suitcase. He's got his best suit, three different ties for different moods and a fake gold pocket watch that he uses when he wants to look impressive. The phone rings. Mr Mountbank fumbles again with the speakerphone button and puts the phone on the bed.

"Little Trixie Worldwide Enterprises."

"Mr Mountbank, this is Zap Zapter calling."

Mr Mountbank freezes. It's a good thing he's not holding the phone or he would have dropped it. "Zap Zapter? *The* Zap Zapter?"

"Yes indeed. I have a business proposal for you."

Mr Mountbank gets a GREEDY RICH GUY look on his face, but then he settles down and just looks kind of sly. "Oh? What kind of business proposal?"

"I'm looking to expand my investments in the publishing sector, and I'm particularly interested in establishing a presence in the southeast. Florida, to be exact."

Now Mr Mountbank is rubbing his hands together. I suppose it's a businessman thing. All he says is, "I see."

"I'd like to schedule a meeting with you for Saturday evening. I'm attending a charity auction in your hometown. I was invited by the President of the Hatahatchee Chamber of Commerce. I understand you're a big wheel in Hatahatchee, so you're already planning to be there, am I right?"

And all Mr Jefferson Mountbank can say is, "Yes. Yes, I will be there."

"Good," says Zap Zapter smoothly. "I'm looking forward to meeting you."

* * *

When Beatrice says, "What if he works it out? I erased his call history so he wouldn't see the number you were calling from, but he might try to look up Zap Zapter's number or something and he'll find out that the real Zap never called him."

With a face full of wisdom and sadness, Folly says, "Trust me. No one who tries to call Zap Zapter actually gets to talk to him."

Act III

SCENE THREE

(Good old Hatahatchee Street.)

It's the day of the auction. Curtain time. Time to leverage our best practices, according to Folly, but I don't have time to think about what that means, because I'm too busy trying to leverage some speed. I'm starting with a chase sequence and it's a good one this time. The sun is shining, but believe it or not, the sun has worked out a way to look menacing as I burst through my front door and take off down the street, past Mr Jameson's house, like Folly chasing after money. I am so speedy, the spotlight couldn't catch me.

Now you catch a look at who's coming after me: it's May. That thing coming off her head is not her own hair, it's Gram's curlicue. The words *I'm going to pull your hair out and see how you like it* get sucked away from her in the wind and spread out over all of Hatahatchee Street.

I head for the only place I know is safe: the Boardroom. I only hope the anti-Pen padlock is off the door, because I won't have time to twist it left-right-left and I don't think I could remember the numbers right now anyway. I can hear the sound of power tools again, so Dad must be working somewhere near by, without a single clue to the danger his only son is in.

Oh, thank the good Lord, the padlock is off and the door is open a crack. I'm going for it. I'm like a bat: give me a quarter-inch and I'll slip through. I can squeeze my body like an octopus does. I can do anything if it means I'm saved.

Just as I reach for the handle, Folly swings the door open all the way and my face gets it from the lock I put on myself last summer. *Whack!* And I'm down.

I think I see angels. There may be bluebirds flying in a circle around my head. That's hard to do in the theatre, but whatever the effects look like, I took a pretty good fall.

"Help me," is all I hear, and I don't know if it's me saying it or someone else.

"Help me get him up." It's Folly. Two sets of hands grab me. One is trying to pull me up, the other is trying to squash me like a palmetto bug, which is just a fancy name for a big old Florida cockroach.

"We ought to pull him up by his hair," says the other set of hands. The other set of hands belongs to May. I recognize the long fingers.

This is how we got here: I asked May, as the tallest Juiceboxer and the one who looks the most like Gram, if she would be Gram's understudy. That means if Gram gets sick again, May goes on in her place. Well, Gram got sick. I wanted to do the nice thing for May, so I brought her Gram's curlicue and Beatrice's nose putty and I even tried to cut her hair a little bit the way Gram does, just to help the resemblance. What she's objecting to is that I did it while she was asleep.

Folly doesn't seem to notice. "You're looking lovely today, May," he whispers over my corpse. "Did you do something with your hair?"

May's answer to Folly is to poke me hard in the cheek. "What were you thinking? Let me answer that for you: nothing. Flies were buzzing around in that brain suitcase of yours while you took a pair of scissors to my hair, which is not just any old hair but an actual asset that I was planning to take out an insurance policy on."

"A wise course of action," says Folly, nodding.

"What am I supposed to insure now? This cheap fake ponytail?" May grabs a handful of curlicue and shakes it at me. I suppose she can't work out how to unclip it from her head.

It's time for me to start talking. "You don't look that bad, May," I say soothingly. "A lot of actors have nice short hair and wear wigs for different roles. It's more practical."

"I don't care about practical," says May. "This hair – no,

not this hair, the other hair, my own hair, which you sawed off – was my trademark. When you see that hair, you're supposed to immediately say, May Camazzola."

"May Camazzola," Folly gurgles.

"Now you want me to go to the theatre looking like this tonight and draw all kinds of attention to myself? I ought to tell you no. I ought to leave you to work this whole thing out on your own. You can pretend to be Gram and wear this on your head and wrap yourself up in a curtain again and I'll laugh at you from the front row."

You already know how things go when I'm wearing a curtain. May has to do this. If she backs out, we're sunk.

I think of what Gram told me about May, how she's afraid to make a fool of herself. And I know what my unique selling proposition is going to be in this sale.

I turn on a smile that even impresses Folly. He gives me a quick nod to show his approval. "Think of it this way, May: it's the role of a lifetime."

"The role of a lifetime is Sierra Boggess playing Christine in *Phantom of the Opera*. Not *me* wearing *this*," May says, shaking the curlicue at me again, "and tripping over myself in shoes that are two sizes too big."

"You always play the princess or the queen, you always wear nice costumes, and everyone gets to see your hair because you always shine it up with Turtle Wax or whatever it is you use. You can't have a career on Broadway only playing pretty people. You have to take a risk sometimes. You need range, May," I say, thinking of what Ruben says about playing whatever part you're cast in, no fussing, because every role is a chance to learn something new.

"I can think of a range of things I'd like to do to you," she growls. "It starts with a pair of hedge clippers and that nest of straw you call your hair." She reaches out and snatches a piece of chicken coop straw from my head, and I start to sweat. There are no lights, and there's no karaoke machine, but this performance is wearing me out.

Enter Folly, in a brave attempt to rescue me. He's not even acting this time, not as Zap Zapter or Zap Junior, or anyone but himself. "Personally, May, I'd pay to watch you tap dance in a rubbish bag."

But May doesn't take this in the spirit in which it's meant. "All right, that's it. You two get out of my sight. Neither of you is helping anything, which shouldn't surprise me. A delinquent hairstylist and an egg salesman. What do I expect? Just get out and let me think about how to fix this mess."

Even though we're already out, since we're standing in the fresh air and sunshine, I take the chance for freedom and scoot away back home with Folly wandering along a few steps behind me.

"Did you hear that, Sid?" he sighs. "She called me a salesman!"

Act III

SCENE FOUR

(*Everyone's gathered at the Juicebox for what I hope will be a resolution and not a catastrophe, at least not the kind of catastrophe we've been having so far.*)

All the kids are waiting with their families, Mum's there in her favourite long white dress, and Miss Alabama Harper has brought a boatload of refreshments.

This time there's not a Hog Farmer to be seen at the concession stand. Folly asked her to make treats with a business theme, and so the table is covered with dozens of little bow-tie-wearing cupcakes. Each one has ZZ written in bright green gel icing, too. "I bet Zap himself would eat a cupcake that looked like this," says Folly, setting up his new sign:

CUPCAKES
Bidding starts at $3.00.

Mr Jameson's there, too, looking sharp in a new suit.

"You said it was a high-society event," he says, wheeling himself up to the concession stand. "I didn't want to disappoint."

I brought the case Mr Jameson gave me and put it on a shelf behind the concession stand. It took all my discipline not to open the case. I just told myself that it was like Pandora's Box, which I actually have a copy of in the prop closet from Myth Week. If you open the box, all the troubles and sorrows of the world come flying out, and I've got enough of those already.

"What's in the case, Sid?" Folly asks.

"The contents of the case are classified," Mr Jameson says. "It's strictly need-to-know."

"And I don't need to know?" says Folly.

"The situation may change," says Mr Jameson. "Sid knows what to do."

"I do?"

"It may be deployed in a true emergency, if it's been authorized."

"By who?" asks Folly.

"By *whom*," is all Mr Jameson says.

Who comes along just then in a dirty dog costume but Francolina, like a prisoner who's taken it in her own paws to free herself. "Frankie! What are you doing here?"

She doesn't answer. I suppose I should've expected that.

"Frankie, sit," I say, and she drops to the floor without a dog-word of protest, but I can tell she was hoping for a bigger role.

Ruben's practising his auctioneer babble, and Pen is in the back row clutching her bottle of pomegranate juice like a dagger. We have a couple of people in the audience who look like they could be Hatahatchee high society. Miss Alabama Harper's wearing a dress that looks like it's made out of those paper things cupcakes come in, and Mum looks elegant, I think, but she's making herself sick running around helping Jelly Baby get packed and making sure the lots are set up for the auction. She stops by Miss Alabama and says, "You should come and do costumes for us, Allie," and Miss Alabama blushes and says she likes Mum's dress, too, which is nothing special if you ask me. It just makes her look even more pale. In fact, she looks like she's coming down with whatever Gram's got.

The person I most want to see is May, who hasn't shown her face since this morning. She didn't want to come in the car with us, so I'm hoping someone on Hatahatchee Street can bring her. Just in case she's coming, I stick my head out the door. The sky is dark with clouds and there's a wind like you only get before a thunderstorm. But I don't see May anywhere.

I suppose if she doesn't show up, I'll be the understudy to the understudy. I'd ask Beatrice, since she's used to the spotlight, but it would look bad to have a kid bidding against her dad.

I'm about to close the door when someone drives up in a shiny purple Land Rover with a bad illustration of Beatrice's face on the side. Mr Mountbank. I wave at Folly, who waves to Beatrice, who comes over near the door.

Mr Mountbank enters.

Beatrice shakes his hand, which is kind of funny, so I laugh. Mr Mountbank snorts, "Who's this?" and Beatrice says with a perfectly straight face, "Oh, he's an orphan. We let him stay here in exchange for working as a stagehand. Come and meet Ruben, Daddy."

"I have important people to meet, Trixie. Zap Zapter himself invited me here. Have you seen him yet?" Mr Mountbank pulls at his tie, and he looks worse at it than Folly does with his bow tie.

"Not yet. Take a look at all the stuff we're auctioning off. I'll get you a cupcake."

Mr Mountbank frowns. He doesn't go to the stage to look everything over but sits down in the front row and taps his foot on the floor. He's wearing those pointy business shoes that even Folly makes fun of. He can't stop looking around him, like Zap Zapter's going to jump on him from behind one of the seats.

"An orphan?" I whisper to Beatrice as she passes by me.

"Yeah, so don't break character. He's got to give money to a place that supports orphans. If you don't do that, you get kicked out of the Kiwanis club."

I grab a broom and start sweeping. "Go and make him look at everything again. He didn't notice the boxes."

Mr Mountbank checks his watch. He snaps his fingers and jerks his head at Beatrice, which must mean he puts her somewhere around waiters and dogs in his scheme of things, and I hear him say loudly, "Don't take any rubbish from that young man at the concession stand. We'll buy a cupcake for two-fifty and that's it. Get two. I want to give one to Zap Zapter when he shows up."

Beatrice goes to the concession stand and plonks down five dollars. She takes two cupcakes. Folly gives her a stern look, but he must realize it's all part of the show, so he doesn't complain.

"Where is old Zap, do you suppose?" Mr Mountbank says when Beatrice comes back. She gives the cupcakes to Mr Mountbank, but he sets them in the empty chair next to him and keeps looking around. He looks almost like Folly does when he's considering how to present May with the twelve perfect eggs he's chosen for her. "I'm having a box delivered here. I want to show him some of our finest stock."

"The Little Trixie stuff?" Beatrice looks disgusted.

"No, not that. It's from my new project."

"From the insect museum in Miami? You're having insects delivered here?"

"What's wrong with that? I think old Zap would be very interested. Where the heck is he, anyway?"

Beatrice, I'm noticing, has transformed herself from plain old Beatrice to BEATRICE, like she's now a character instead of just an ordinary person with ordinary things to say. Now she's got a purpose and a motivation and an action and all that stuff. You can see it in her eyes. She swoops right into her role and says:

Oh, Dad, I meant to tell you. Zap Zapter was here, but he had to leave for a second.

(What's going on behind Mr Mountbank is Frankie's seen the cupcakes, and she's sneaking up on them. This is so good, I'm just going to have to let her go for it.)

"He had to leave?" says Mr Mountbank. "But he'll be back?"

BEATRICE

Sure, he'll be back.

(Frankie is making use of that long pink tongue of hers and licking all the bow-tie frosting off Mr Mountbank's cupcake and Zap Zapter's, too.)

(Lick.)

BEATRICE

In fact, before he left, he said he was looking forward to meeting you.

(Lick.)

"He said that?" Mr Mountbank goes bright red.

(Lick.)

BEATRICE

Yes indeed. In fact—

And this is where BEATRICE gets interrupted from her second *In fact* because now her dad has gone the colour of his purple Land Rover and is pointing in Frankie's direction.

"What is that mutt doing here? I'll tell you what it's doing here, it's eating my corporate gift to Zap Zapter. That's what it's doing. Why, if I ran this place, I'd tell a dog like that–"

BEATRICE takes one look at Frankie's frosted snout and, just like she's taking on Folly in a smooth-talking competition, she says:

That's Zap Zapter's dog. Argos is his name. Haven't you ever seen a photograph of Zap and his dog?

And what can Mr Mountbank say but, "Well, sure I have. Of course I have. Argos . . . A fine name for a dog! I guess old Zap won't mind if his very own dog licks his cupcake, will he?" He gives Frankie a little pat on the nose and smiles at her, now that she's official royalty.

(BEATRICE looks relieved. I think she wore herself out with that improvisation, so I'm going to let her just be Beatrice again.)

I'm trying to signal to Beatrice to get her dad to take another look at the stage so he'll notice the box and get filled with fear. Mr Mountbank isn't looking fearful, just impatient. Even Argos, who has decided to fall asleep on Mr Mountbank's pointy shoe, isn't enough to distract him from the fact that Zap Zapter still has not shown his famous face.

Folly says the cupcake bidding isn't going very well, since there are about ninety cupcakes, and if you don't bid first on one, you can always bid first on another.

"Scarcity," he says. "I should have known."

Since there's still no sign of May, it's time for me to swallow my pride and get ready to play the mystery bidder. All I need is a good hat and maybe some make-up, and since I don't know how to do that myself, I swallow some more pride and ask Beatrice.

She stares at me like I'm a blank wall that needs paint. "Good thing you have that bruise already. That'll help. Let's give you a little dirt, too."

"Dirt? Why dirt?"

"You're an orphan, aren't you? All our orphans get dirt on their faces."

And before I can say that there's a difference between a stage orphan and a real orphan, which is what I suppose I'm supposed to be, living in the Florida panhandle in the twenty-first century and not in a London sewer way back then, she takes a make-up compact out of her pocket and starts brushing my cheeks.

Jelly Baby has stayed up in Ruben's apartment getting the S.W.I.Z. crate ready to go, but now she comes down just in time to see Beatrice pulling at my hair and rubbing a little gel in it to make it stick up funny.

"That looks better than your real hair," says Jelly Baby, and Beatrice makes me turn around for inspection.

"Not bad," she says.

"Too bad you don't have time to make him a papier-mâché cast for his leg or something," says Jelly Baby.

"I do like making things out of papier-mâché," says Beatrice, and she giggles.

She goes to her dad and leads him over to the stage, pretending that she's fussing over an alligator-skin footstool that looks like something Gram would wear on her head. And then it happens: Mr Mountbank kind of jumps as he sees the Little Trixie boxes, and he goes to Ruben right away. Maybe he's going to try to buy them flat out, and he'll pay enough that I won't have to worry about playing the filthy mystery orphan with enough money to buy something at an auction.

They talk a good long while. Mr Mountbank waves his arms, and Ruben is standing the way he usually does when someone's parents are complaining that their kid didn't get a big enough part, or a good enough costume, or whatever. Then he catches my eye and bobs his head, and I know that means I have to come over. Well, if I have to go anywhere near Mr Mountbank, I'm taking Folly with me.

"Boys," says Ruben when we've finally made the long

231

trek across the carpet, "there seems to be a problem with the items you donated to the auction. Mr Mountbank is saying that they belong to him."

"Oh, no," says Folly, putting on his best Boy Scout, "those office supplies were sent to us in the post, as card-carrying members of the Little Trixie Commerce Club. It's the property of King and Camazzola, and as you can see, it says Marked for Destruction, so if it ever did belong to Mr Mountbank, he must not have wanted it very much."

Mr Mountbank makes a noise in the back of his throat. "Rubbish!" he says, and then he glares at me. "You're that orphan Trixie pointed out to me, and I don't know if the word of a child without reputable parents can ever be trusted."

What can I say to that? Ruben shoots me a look that's about to give the game away, so I jump in and hope he knows Folly's rule about selling property. I know he knows that when an actor is on a roll, you have to just let them go for it.

"Ever since my parents died in the cracker factory explosion, I've had to support myself," I say. "But I wouldn't ever do anything illegal. Orphans get extra-long prison sentences if they break the law in Florida. It's true. I read it on the back of a cereal box once. I mean, a cereal box I found in the rubbish while I was digging through it to get at some old stale doughnuts someone threw away so I could have something to eat for the first time in four days. That happens all the time. And – and sometimes when I'm

232

digging through the rubbish I get bitten by cockroaches, that's how bad it is, but I still wouldn't stoop to breaking the law."

"Cockroaches don't generally bite human beings, and I don't see what that has to do with my records being your personal property," Mr Mountbank says, and that's when I start talking even faster.

"You tell that to my parents after they died of rare Panhandle Biting Cockroach bites. It was awful. That's the most poisonous insect in all Florida. Or is it venomous? I can't ever remember."

"Venomous," says Mr Mountbank. "And the most venomous insect in Florida is the fire ant, but it's hardly fatal. I'm having some sent here this afternoon, as a matter of fact. But I thought your parents died in a cracker factory explosion."

"Oh, they did, but there were a lot of biting cockroaches at the cracker factory, and, uh–"

Now Ruben steps in. "Why are you having venomously poisonous insects delivered to my children's theatre?"

Mr Mountbank stammers, "Well, they're not for the children. They're for Zap Zapter. They're for him to see. I think he'll want to invest in my – well, never mind about that. The point here is that these boxes are coming with me, and if you're going to argue with me about it, I can call a lawyer faster than he can grab a doughnut out of the rubbish." He jabs a thumb in my direction.

I can tell Ruben's disappointed. "I'll keep these boxes

backstage and perhaps we can work out this disagreement afterwards. Boys, I'm sorry I can't take your donation. And Mr Mountbank, I hope you'll find something here worth bidding on to support your daughter's love of the theatre."

"A waste of time," says Mr Mountbank. "Just like I've always said."

By this time, Mum's feeling so weak, she goes backstage to rest, and Jelly Baby asks me if I can help get her costume ready. Not a puppet's costume. Her costume. She's acting, and Beatrice is operating a puppet. The craziest part of it is that it was Beatrice's idea. When Jelly Baby told her about her great-grandfather and how a puppet had special status and could tease a king, Beatrice said, "I'll tease him, all right," and that was that.

Since I'm no good with costumes, Miss Alabama Harper offers to step in. She already knows about most of our plan, but I explain about the *Hamlet* idea, and she gets it immediately.

"'The play's the thing,'" she says, "'wherein I'll catch the conscience of the King'." The way she says it, I can tell it's a quote.

"I'll catch his conscience, all right," says Beatrice darkly, and I can see she's really getting into this role.

Miss Alabama rustles off backstage in her cupcake dress, taking Jelly Baby and Beatrice with her. "I'll see how your mum's doing, too," she says to me. "Maybe she needs a blanket or something."

Frankie gets up and follows them backstage, and Mr

Mountbank looks relieved, even if he thought it was Zap Zapter's dog licking his cupcake and sleeping on his shoes.

After a minute, Beatrice signals to Ruben to turn the house lights down. Everyone in the audience takes a seat. I sit near Folly and Mr Jameson at the concession stand.

Jelly Baby comes out dressed in Beatrice's Martina the Cockroach costume, minus the paper bags on each of her legs. She struts around, being a beautiful cockroach, and the audience laughs, and then Beatrice comes out with the clown marionette. I'm not saying that clown looks just like Beatrice when she's dressed up as a Little Trixie clown, but . . . okay, I am saying that. It's like Beatrice is leading a little version of herself around on strings.

In a loud, stagey voice, Jelly Baby announces, "Watch this. I'm going to get some money out of this clown." She leans down and holds out her hand. "I can make you rich. If you give me money today, you'll get four times as much back tomorrow."

The marionette lifts its arm up like it's putting something in the cockroach's hand. The cockroach shows the audience the imaginary money and then slides it inside the costume while the clown does a little dance, not seeing what the cockroach has done. Then the clown holds out its hand to get paid back, and the cockroach makes a big "I don't know what happened to it" kind of gesture, and the audience laughs again.

A groan comes from backstage. That's not part of the show. That's my mum. She must be feeling terrible.

The cockroach and the clown repeat this little scene three more times – the clown gives the cockroach money, the cockroach hides it, and then the cockroach acts like nothing happened. I watch Mr Mountbank to see if he's looking remorseful or guilty or anything, but he just looks impatient. My mum groans again from backstage, and I wish Miss Alabama would just take her home.

Finally, the clown stamps its foot. Beatrice must have practised hard, because she's good at operating the marionette. Better than she is at acting, anyway. I watched the two of them run through the show a couple of times, and I love what comes next: the clown chases the cockroach, even though the clown is tiny and the cockroach is huge, and they go around and around the stage until the cockroach takes all the money out of its costume (real money this time, put there before the show started), throws it at the clown, and runs offstage.

They start going, with Jelly Baby taking little steps and the clown taking big steps, and they go faster and faster. The audience loves it, even if it's not making Mr Mountbank run for the exit out of shame.

Just as Jelly Baby's getting ready to take the money out of her costume, two delivery men come out from stage right, wheeling a crate on a dolly. The crate says *S.W.I.Z.* in red stencils. The men, who are wearing blue striped overalls and caps like old-fashioned train conductors, blink under the lights and say, "Whoops." If these are the men who came to take Doña Flor away, they got lost on the way out. I don't know if I'd trust them with a priceless heirloom – or a box of old ledgers, to be honest. They look pretty short, and they're not very organized.

"Let's see," one of them says. "Which is the way out?"

Mr Mountbank is suddenly very interested in what's happening onstage. He jumps up and shouts, "Leave it right there, fellas. Leave it right there! Oh, boy!" He rubs his hands together again. "Just wait till Zap gets here to see this!" He climbs onto the stage and strides over to the crate.

The delivery men look at each other, shrug and walk offstage.

"Daddy!" cries Beatrice. "You ruined our show! We were just about to finish it."

"Listen, Trixie, this is an important opportunity for me," says Mr Mountbank. "You wouldn't want your old dad to miss out on a chance to impress Zap Zapter, would you? Of course not! I'm going to check on the cargo here to make sure everything's shipshape, and then – and then –" Mr Mountbank is trying to pry the front of the crate open, but he can't get a grip on it. He pulls and grunts, and then suddenly there's a crowbar in his hand, like someone just handed it to him out of the prop closet. "Now we're in business!"

He starts prying and bashing the crate with the crowbar, and then Ruben walks onstage and puts a hand on Mr Mountbank's shoulder.

"Sir, I–"

Mr Mountbank spins around. "Zap? Mr Zapter?" He shields his eyes from the lights. "Oh, you're not Zap. Just let me get ready here. I'm sure Zap will be along any minute. I've got a heck of an idea here, if you don't mind me saying it. It's going to be a hit and a half. Kids will love it. I said to myself, what do kids love more than anything? More than reading? Why, insects, of course! What kid doesn't love insects, as I do myself? I've taken the liberty of having some of our best rare insects shipped here tonight to show old Zap, and I think he's going to be my number one investor."

Mr Mountbank is waving the crowbar around, he's getting so excited, and I can see Ruben's looking for an opportunity to take it out of his hands without getting whacked in the face. But then the focus of the scene changes. I'm not going to draw it for you. I don't think I could.

The side door flings open, letting in driving rain and a flash of lightning, and someone screeches, "Is the auction over?" I twist to see, and my heart does something it has never done before: it leaps at the sight of soaking-wet May, dressed in purple and orange and yellow. That's Mr Jameson's second-favourite thing in the whole world wrapped around her neck, only on May right now it looks as bedraggled as the rest of her, and I have to check Mr Jameson to make sure he's not rolling over there to mow her down. I know she took his eggs, but how did she get that scarf?

Mr Jameson looks all right, though. He's even got a little smile on.

The curlicue looks even worse on May now than it did before, like a platinum blonde toilet brush of hair. She steps forward and stumbles, and I see she's even shoved her feet into those dog-chewed orange high heels. She must've dug that shoe out of the dirt in Folly's garden for this.

"She looks like she's beaten up six different old ladies and taken their clothes," says Folly.

"She looks like karaoke night set on fire," says Mr Jameson.

Oh, May. You are one of the great ladies of the theatre.

Following May is Folly's mum, looking a lot more put together but just as wet. Folly's face breaks open into the best smile I've ever seen. Pure Folly. Mrs King comes over to us and puts her arms around Folly. He whispers something to her, and she nods and says, "I know, honey. I know."

May rushes up to the stage with Pen close behind her at the same time that Mum comes out of the wings, pale and sweaty and yanking on Frankie's lead to keep her from jumping all over that orange clown.

Mr Mountbank turns to stare at May, too, but he's forgotten that he still has the crowbar in his hands, and he swings it *smash* into the front of the crate, which must be badly made for a box that's supposed to keep things from getting broken, because it comes open, the giant puppet tumbles forward, and as Mr Mountbank swings around the other way to smile at Argos and everyone ducks, the crowbar goes straight into Doña Flor's cheek. Her red, rosy, papier-mâché cheek. Part of the packing case hits Pen in the arm, and she squeezes the bottle of juice, which sprays all over the front of Mum's white dress.

Mum groans, "Oooohhhhh!" and trips over Frankie's lead and gets it caught around her ankle, so it makes a clanking sound when she moves. She catches Frankie behind the ears on her way down to the floor. Frankie takes her cue, collapsing on top of Mum like Argos on a pile of manure.

Jelly Baby gasps.

"What – what are you–" She's frozen. Beatrice is frozen, the clown marionette is frozen, Mr Mountbank's frozen. It's like they're doing an exercise, and someone's posed them like this, and everyone else has to guess what's happening in this scene. Mr Mountbank just babbles. "I – it was – insects, you know, and – Zap Zapter – he was – I don't know what–"

From underneath Frankie, Mum groans, "What does your conscience tell you to do?"

Mrs King is looking around the concession stand. "Someone ought to check on your mum, Sid," she says. "Do you have a first-aid kit? She might have cut herself in that fall."

"Yeah, there's a white plastic box on one of those shelves with some bandages and stuff," says Folly. "Here." He reaches for a box and hands it to his mum. She runs up to the stage before I think to tell her she's not holding a first-aid kit.

That's Mr Jameson's case. I know he's a practical man, but I'm betting his lucky award isn't a box of plasters. I follow Mrs King, and Folly follows me. Mr Jameson stays put, like he's just enjoying the show.

"Just hold still," says Mrs King to my mum, trying to untangle her from Frankie's lead. Mum does have a little scratch on her finger.

Mrs King pops open the latch on the case and looks puzzled.

At the same time, and in the same holy voice, Folly and Mr Mountbank whisper, "The Golden Bow Tie."

And I see that Mr Jameson knows something about being a prop master, too. I step up and take the case from Mrs King. "Yes, sir," I say, showing Mr Jameson's Golden Bow Tie award all around. "This is the highest honour Zap Zapter can bestow upon any individual. For, uh, service to insects and zoos, and, uh–"

Folly jumps in. "For business ethics. Since you were about to make a handsome payment for damages to this priceless antique and a donation to the arts. Weren't you, sir?"

Mr Mountbank looks baffled. He must think Mrs King is Zap Zapter's personal representative, because he says to her, "Of course I'll pay for damages, I mean, well, business ethics – Golden Bow Tie! – and I, I'm honoured to receive

241

it, and you can tell Zap that I've always thought the theatre was a viable business model–"

Mrs King cuts him off. "It doesn't matter if it's a viable business model or not, Mr Mountbank," she says smoothly. Now I see where Folly gets it. "Not everything is about money. The theatre is part of our common humanity, and as such, it takes common humanity like us to protect it."

"Just as I've always said," says Mr Mountbank sadly, and Pen chooses that moment to throw the rest of her pomegranate juice at him.

* * *

You almost have the whole picture. I think I can squeeze everything else into just one more scene.